I0520148

Life's Heart Break

A Novella

Books by the Anonymous Author and Artist

Duty and Destruction I

A real female experiences life in and out of the U.S. military.

Life's Poetic Dichotomies

Some of life's biggest dichotomies are juxtaposed poetically.

Her Poetic Rise

It is for the religiously poetic that blends religion and feminism.

Life's Short Stories

Fictional characters vie to live their own lives.

Life's Mixed Poetry

Poems are mixed schematically, stylistically, and randomly.

Life's Novellas: Fate Waits Upon No One

The good and the bad are juxtaposed, chronologically, fictionally, and theatrically.

Their Poetic Minds

Poems are juxtaposed, religiously, femininely, and dichotomously.

Poems of Life

Poems are mixed schematically, stylistically, and randomly.

Art Book

The Diamond & Heart Art Collections

Pictures are exhibited, categorically, by coloring schemes and coloring mediums; all of which, have been affected with special effects.

Schemes: pastel shades; earth tones; primary colors; gray, black and white; black and white.

Mediums: colored pencils; water coloring; pastel coloring; acrylic coloring; oil coloring.

Life's Heart Break

A Novella

Anonymous

Century Conquests

Life's Heart Break

A Novella

Copyright © 2013 by Anonymous

www.centuryconquests.com
info@centuryconquests.com

ISBN: 978-0-9850698-9-6

Cover graphic designed by: Century Conquests © 2013

Century Conquests ® 2012

Life's Heart Break

A Novella

Anonymous

Acknowledgements

Yet, again, for the small voice deep in me that wants me to carry on fictionally.

I thank every single person, also, that has helped with the publication of this book.

I thank, too, every single reader of my book, for permitting me the privilege of engaging, engrossing, and enlightening you.

Author's Note

This is a work of fiction. In addition, and, so assuming no responsibility for any figurative or even literal mix-up; best efforts have been put forth; to just actualize, the historical, cultural, social, religious, political, and the like; references, inferences, interpretations, and so forth—or, forces, that are contained here in.

Additionally, the publisher and the author both have had no necessary need to denigrate any ("so-called, or otherwise"), human figure; or, a company's product; or even, its service; and so on, except, in the case of actual necessity.

Hearts and Flowers
(A Villanelle)

Wouldn't life be just great without any heart-breakers and
heart-break?
Yet, life could—or, would nev'r be so damn kind, to grant
the hearty a promisingly pang-less love;
Whose circularly, if not colorfully dark composition
encompasses much color.
Such dark coloring, almost, always, to a great extent,
covers up the hearty's emotional distress.
That, often times, causes the hearty to rove:
Roving, roundly, if not waveringly, in a pretty pitch-black-
color'd lake full of Heart-Ache.
Needless to say, that, it can be an utterly un-pretty process:
Or, roaming, darkly, if not ditheringly, can't—and, most
likely, won't be enough, ev'r; to put the hearty back into
the above.
But, instead, the hearty is left, quite simply, forsaken:
breaking, and aching, and even hating another or some
other.
Needless to say, again, that, it can be an utterly un-pretty
process, or, a sure lack of success;
Or better, roving, un-colorfully, if not blunderingly; right,
in an un-joyously jet-black-color'd lake full of lovelessly
blackish-blue-color'd, and love-sick, and ev'n hard-heart'd
doves.
All is surely, enough, too, to make the hearty shriek, so
soundly, with sorrow, that'll more than likely be present
tomorrow; like, a fantastically, if not, a fabulously fake date
of a mate that's been—of course, right, on the take.
Thus, having been such, what's the hearty's course of
recourse, or real redress?

Could or should the hearty just link to, or shrivel from, or
ev'n sink into some shrinkingly bluish-black-color'd
gloves;
Whose un-colorful color could—or, would serve—only, to
cloud the un-belov'd hearty's pretty un-propitious pother.
That, such damnably dark coloring of a cloud, almost,
nev'r, precipitate or perpetuate any proper progress.
Like, a grief-stricken, heart-broken, and mid-night-black-
color'd bird of a lonesome dove; that's confin'd, and
circularly, to a suffocatingly empty tub.
It's ev'n a place or a super small space, where wickedly
wishful love is only placat'd with much mud—then,
vacat'd.
Will the hearty—or, better yet, he just heed the wonderfully
wise words of a warning from his wonderful mother?

A.

Part I

The Zolden Family

Love, like fortune turns upon a wheel, and is very much
given to rising and falling.

—Sir John Vsnbrugh
(1664-1726)

Naples, Florida
Early Spring, 2008
Sunday Brunch

It is very true is it not?

I'm talking about Sir John Vsnbrugh (1664-1726), having said—that, "'Love, like fortune turns upon a wheel, and is very much given to rising and falling.'" How many damn times in the past that I've been at love's high-end—only, at the end of the day, to end up at its low-end: single, still? I'm just so damned tired of greeting or meeting utterly undesirable or fantastically fallible females.

Sitting, here, at one of six spacious patio tables—or, in the most spacious of seats that're spaced, so, spaciously; I glance at the scuba diver's watch that's on my right wrist. It's nearing 11:30 a.m., on a goldenly gorgeous and Sunday morning.

Next, I fire up my poison. After having come over to my parents' home some 15 or 20 minutes ago; and, then, having entered the house with my personal house-key; I've since settled on the pool deck of a terrace.... It's a life-size place, or a full-scale space that's like a sanctuary, or a safe haven. I'm even a bit embarrassed to say so, too. That, I've needed some protection from the very likes of female users, and, mis-users, and, even, abusers, or, goddamned losers...! Steady.

Flavoring a long-drawn-out swallow of my drink..., I just want it through before long.... It and my costly cigar both are just keeping me company, most comfortably, amid my waiting.... Speaking of those damned abusers, and mis-users, and even users, or god-damned losers; my mother—or, *Zakira*, almost, always, gives me very good advice, and, rightly, relating to the damned female-eat-male struggle, or fight. That's right. She's my personal advisor of sort. My father, or Zack and *Zakira* both should be joining me here, or out-doors, and, soon. Since, our usual family brunch of a roundly robust rite—or, ritual, begins right at 12:00 p.m., sharp, supposedly. Most, likely, that my dad and my mom both are right up-stairs…, still, preparing for such; which is why, upon my arrival, I just let them be. Or, I've been free to smoke, drink, and relax, some.

Now, of course, every single thing has since been set, right, by *Zakira*, her-self. My parents have an excellent personal chef—Mister *Soo Sung*; who works a few days a week or so…, here. Though, *Zakira* appreciates, absolutely, fixing our very own family brunch or lunch…, and all. Or, so she says…, although *Soo Sung* tends to assist … in some way or another way, quite presumably.

My only sister, or Zara should be here…, soon, too. Her husband—Rex, more often than not, is almost always the cause of Zara's often in-apt in-punctuality. Since, they don't exactly be late. But, instead, the twosome so typically arrives round about the right time or not necessarily early.

I continue puffing on my poisonously sweet cigar, and savoring a super stretched-out swallow of my circularly crisp Chivas Regal. I even look over at the out-door kitchen where upon some more liquor awaits me so very patiently. Then, I just decide not to indulge its patience or semi-open invitation.

Yet, what I'll indulge—or, entertain, right, quick, is the thought of my impendent business trip plus romantic rendezvous. That, I'll be indulging, tomorrow, and, rather, pleasurably. More, I'm some-what reluctant to tell *Zakira* about my plan to meet Ms. Caren Colson….

She and I both met some time ago, on-line. Or, most pointedly, we've since hooked right up, at Realty Romance: or, a roundly romantic web-site for realtors. That's correct.

As, I'm not only President and Chief Operating Officer, (or COO), of Zolden Enterprises, Incorporated: (or, a big real estate, conglomerate); But, also, I'm one of its most hard-working and fun-loving realtors—and, brokers: Ha-Ha-Ha!

One of the things that I quite appreciate about on-line dating is its circularly colorful, (or, even, its circularly un-colorful) convenience. Though, my romantic preference is to first meet a lady or a woman, up close, or, in person. Since, I'll just know—right, away, if there's any physical attraction or the lack thereof.

Now, this isn't to say, that, mental, and, emotional, and, even, spiritual connections aren't very important. But, I'll most likely find it very difficult, at best, or worst, pretty impossible; to lie next to, or lie down with a female, that I don't even want to touch; and, that I don't even want to touch me. I suppose, as well, that it's a good if not a great thing. That, the best or wisest way to a lady's heart is right through her mind, heart, and spirit, and not her body, or her bed....

Naturally, my mother has inculcated such wisdom in me for as long as I can or care to remember. Actually, it's how, exactly, that *Zakira* has captured her husband's or my father's very spirit, and heart, and even mind: right, by wowing him, intellectually, morally, and spiritually; which, among some other things, encircles so very much, more...: academically, ethically, and so forth.

Once, again, I glance at the *Omega*—or, the deep scuba diver's watch that's on my right wrist. Right, now, I'm seeing that it's nearing 12:00 p.m. I'd better finish my poison—relaxing, or drinking, and smoking. Since, I don't want, or need, to hear anyone's circular criticism.... Even, though, just, about every person in this world has some sort of questionable vice or prop or even crutch; and whether or not such is considered nice or even all right: like, brains, or, guts, or, sports, or, looks, or, food-stuffs, or, cigarettes, or, intoxicated drinks, or, drugs, or sexual contacts, or religious beliefs, or support groups, or walkers, or even canes, and so on.

Before it kills me, I go ahead and just kill my cigar in a glassy ash-tray that's atop the glassily clear patio table; whose sensationally sunny bouquet of sun flowers and all are just shining away. They're doing so, right, on a bold or bright and balmy day. There's not one iota or jot of decay, any where. Or, no where in the pool-deck's garden or lot is there any rot.

An array of richly multi-colored flowers, or roses, carnations, and all, just, abound, around, most colorfully, if not, quite beautifully. Right, amid the flowers' beauty are some very emerald-colored plants; whose neighboring and roundly reddish-orange-colored mulch just adds even more colorful beauty; right, to an already and brightly beauteous back-drop, or scene.

I'm even seeing the glitteriest of diamonds. That're glittering atop the pool's water…, or glittering beneath the super shimmery sun-light. If Caren Colson turns right out to be the woman or the lady of my most delicious dream, or even the great love of my life; I'll present her right with a super sparkler, that's sparkling from here to eternity. Plus, some pretty pristine or some pretty pink pearls may even be forth-coming….

Now, I'm through with my pretty potent poisons or roundly relaxant relaxants. I thus push the empty glass and the smelly as well as messy ash-tray—both, aside. Again, I can do without anyone's poisonous criticism…, criticizing, poisonously, my little descent into a damnably dark abyss of a hell. Steady now.

Having walked right over to the open-air of an out-spaced kitchen; I'm now emptying, and cleaning, and even putting away the remnants, or the tall tell-tale signs of my dark decadence. More, if I desire a little more poison, such wouldn't be exactly forth-coming, not here, and, not now. It's because my sister or Zara is now stepping steadily onto the pool deck. She's doing such, in a sexily smart sundress; whose brown color is matching perfectly with her shoes, or pumps.

Not, surprising, either, is that my only 35-year-old sister is just as good-looking as our mother, *Zakira*. Since, *Zakira* has instilled, almost, always, in her children…: the very value of a pretty positive attitude; a very proper diet; some very proper exercise; some very proper rest, and the like; all of which, can and will lead—only, to having more hope, faith, and, ambition, and, even, strength, or, staying power—*personal power*: or, a most meaningful measure of peace, health, love, and, happiness, and even, success; none of which, can almost never be had, ever, without a very circular commitment to, perseverance in, and colorful, or un-colorful courage; rightly, to just with-stand some much higher principle in life other than one's own self-imposed; and, self-styled; and, self-appointed philosophy of life; and, even, the methodology by which such life is lived, worked, or played, poisonously, or not.

That's correct or so right. It's all about out-playing, and out-working, and even out-lasting—all, that would take me—or, us, way down; right, to a nakedly or a starkly dark, deep, cold, dirty, and, shaky, and even, dangerous, or even, deathly ground, floundering, fantastically. So, where, could or would any honor come from in the midst of such super sub-standard-ness? Huh? For, there are some very serious standards, which must be adhered to, without end.

"Hey Bro!" exclaims Zara, smilingly; "Let's go! Or, let's get this brunch or lunch started...!" and moving right toward me in a pair of dark brown-shaded, low-heeled, and leathery-looking pumps, shoes. It's one of my sister's most favorite colors, "brown." She claims that it's an extremely equable color. My most favorite color is none other than basic black. Plus, my claim is that such color doesn't attract evil, but, instead, repels it. That's right or so correct.... The color of basic black can be about what's good as opposed to what's bad or what's sad. And, I'm even glad that it's so. Naturally, I'm just dressed in an off-black and silk-like yet simple slack set with black leather shoes.

Zara and I both meet up, at the front of the pool's deck. It's where I just sat, earlier, relaxing, so poisonously. Though, patio tables with 100% matchable chairs, chaises, and all, are all spaced spaciously or sporadically; the end of the pool is considered, still, where the garden, flowers, and plants, and even water fall all are. Most, cheerfully, cheek-to-cheek, we kiss, or Zara and I, both. Then, we so embrace each other, or even hug, and, lovingly, if not, supportingly, or, quite supposedly.

Now, so disengaging..., "I still want and need all of your support—or, for you to back me—up, concerning the multi-family complex that's on the Palm Coast. Where, too, I'll be visiting tomorrow for a few days...."

"Yeah, and not that you ever need my say-so or go-ahead—since, you're President—or, COO, and all—"

"I know that—but, well, Dad wants us to be extra or very cautious about Zolden Enterprises…, or the family's investment—portfolio, concerning any new real estate…."

"Might I've a little something," Zara says to me, "to wet my tongue, like a quick shot of something, Rum."

Now she's scurrying right to the very well-stocked and out-door bar…. I my-self just scurry right behind Zara with some due speed. Since, my dad and my mom both will be outdoors—only, too, soon. "Hey, Sis…!" I state, a little louder…; "you're Executive Treasurer—so, of course, your financial opinion—most certainly, means something…."

"Thanks Bro…!" replies Zara, and now reaching the kitchenette. She's just about to indulge that drink or some Rum. Carrying on…, "Even though, the market is crashing, and, hard, now isn't the time to just lie back. Or, just, back away, in any way, what so ever, just, like a super scaredy-cat or a black blind bat."

I concur, circularly, if not colorfully, "You're right, quite definitely! I've to just convince Zack—or Dad, to just trust my basic or sensible or even serious instinct, and all."

"Yeah," says Zara, flavoring, or savoring her poison of a drink, Rum; "Well, good luck with that, expanding the empire. And, what's it all about—"

Naturally, it's a very nice-sized, well-occupied, and a properly, or an utterly un-pricey property…."

Zara mutters, "Uhh-huh…," and then comments…, looking round about: "My hubby or Rex should be joining us, outdoors. He wanted to first make some phone call or another—business, as usual."

I now question, curiously, "Why's Rex competing, seemingly, against Zolden Enterprises…? Or, why doesn't he just join our family business—"

"Ahh, well, Rex truly swears by and believes in his independence or autonomy."

"Uh-huh, which is to say, that he doesn't want to be regarded as any sort of mooch or leech?"

"That's right…!" exclaims Zara, and taking another elongated swallow of her poison. She does so, right, before speaking, and interestingly, "listen—here, I just let my man where his pretty paternal pants."

Now isn't the time—or place, to analyze or criticize or patronize or even ostracize my baby sister, Zara. Since, there'll be plenty time to check out what's in her mind, or head, truly. Like, why she's been so pressured by him—or Rex, to have a baby so very soon after marriage…? Such references, and, inferences, and, even, conclusions, have all been Freudian slips…, so to speak, by *Zakira*—my mother; who ought to be joining Zara and me both, outside, SOON. For, it's almost that time, or, 12:00 p.m.

…However, not, at all, before my actually tall and, so physically muscled, and even naturally tannish, or thirty-something, brother-in-law; who's now joining us, Zara and me. Very, interestingly, too, that, as soon as Zara sees Rex coming, she puts away that poison of hers in a big hurry…. She's placing it way below the outdoor kitchen's counter into a drawer of sort.

"Good morning my Brother!" yells Rex, stepping, forwardly, in a pair of gray, leathery, and low-heeled shoes. He's even dressed in the color of gray: silkily mid-sleeved shirt; very well-fitted gabardine, pants, and all. It's his most favorite color—or, gray, per chance. Perhaps, Rex just likes existing in a gray area or even in the gray yonder.

There, in the gray—or distance, he, almost, always, contrives some very interesting if not some unusual ideas.

Just, like his nakedly noble—yet, wildly warped notion of autonomy, or independence…. How is it possible, ever, to be married to someone while being strictly independent of her or him? Huh? If you're to ask me…, I'll tell you, most probably, that such thought is ridiculous, and roundly.

Rex and I or we both just greet each other and then just shake hands, man-to-man. "How've you been doing…, really, Man?" asks Rex, and seemingly, quite smilingly, or rather grinningly.

"I've been all right and you?"

"Oh, well, I can't or won't even complain, for life's pretty good…, and all," replies Rex, and reaching right out for his wife: or, the supposedly great love of his life, Zara Zina Zolden Rayland. She's now joining the both of us, or Rex and me…. Where, we've since met up, or near the big buffet-table, and all. Again, all has been set, already: table, chairs, hot food, cold drinks, and so forth. That is, every single thing is right in its proper place, or secured. The food stuff is secured in stainless steel, containers, and so on.

They hug and then kiss, somewhat, passionately, on the outside, of course. Before dis-engaging, Zara queries or pries: "How did that phone call go—Babe?"

"Oh! Not, to worry, at all—*Luv*, because I've since squared things right away…," he answers, and, smirkingly, right, on the surface. "I've secured yet another contract for my advertising and marketing business—or, Rayland's Ads & All."

"That's just fantastic—Babe…!" Zara exclaims, and hugging, and even kissing her husband, rather passionately, on the exterior.

"So, tell me, Rex," I interpolate, pryingly, "when's your company going to do more advertising and marketing for Zolden Enterprises? Since, I just may've a Palm Coast, property, for you—"

"Hey...!" Rex replies and then inquires, insidiously; "It's not a problem..., making merry, or making merrier.... Incidentally, when's a smart, strong, and, successful, or, a single and even eligible bachelor like you getting married, and all, uh?"

"Please, just, don't start with or worry about me..., Bro. Since, something's been cookin', slowly, and nicely, 'at least, this is my very high hope—'"

"Oh?" Rex remarks, with surprise registering right on his round face...; whose hairy brows are up, and, way; whose brownish-green eyes are open, and, so wide; whose pointy nose is puckered, and, un-prettily; whose big mouth is just about to speak, most, seemingly: "So, you're dating, Bro? Good! Or, GREAT! ...You've since found a mate.... With any luck, for your sake—that, she'll be a beautifully sweet piece of cake instead of a fake..., who'll never make you ache." Continuing, poetically, yet unromantically, "Or, be too damn late with you-all's roundly, if not rapturously romantic date with fate. Or, even, use you as some sort of pretty pricey rake that you'll hate," winking, superficially.

"Naw," I remark, simply, or un-colorfully, and then exclaim, quite colorfully, "for it's all good or great...!"

"All right, Man, if you say so."

Zara has only stood by, so silently, and smilingly, or submissively, while Rex—or, her husband of an advertiser or marketer makes nice: or, advertises..., or, even, markets something or another.... But, what exactly...? The two, or Rex and Zara—both, just kiss and hug, all over again. They stop only because of a rather welcoming intrusion.

Good! The other two are now joining us outdoors. Never mind, too, that they're a wee-bit late for our family lunch or brunch of a joyous date; which almost never can be vacated, (according, to my mother, or *Zakira*). It's just about to be baked, most tastily, or joyously, with some fun and love or hard love yet, still, affection, if not perfection.

Externally, they're a very stylish, sixty-something, and, pretty powerful, and, even, perfect-looking couple: or, the Black-American and Full-Blooded Indian; or, even, Mr. and Mrs. Zack Zolden…: The current Chairman and Chief Executive Officer of Zolden Enterprises—(Zack), coupled with its current Executive Secretary—(or, *Zakira*). That's correct, right! They're pretty perfect—all right, or, almost, always.

My handsome father is stepping steadily toward us. He's dressed casually yet chicly and colorfully. He's doing so, or stepping, in a very new-looking, and well-fitting, and even light-maroon-colored slack-set of sort; whose lightly woolen shirt is just matching quite nicely with its slightly wide pants; whose very slight flare is failing, and rightly, to cover up some sturdily leathern shoes.

My beautiful mother is stepping steadily toward us, as well. She's just dressed casually yet stylishly and rather colorfully. The beautifully Indian-styled, and very velvety-looking, and even medium-length—or, the richly inherited skirt-set is more of a striking sight for dull eyes. With terra-cotta-colored fringes, having been sewn strategically about the dark turquoise-colored and V-shaped blouse's bottom sleeves; and, even, having been sewn strategically about the form-fitting skirt's very bottom hem; all is very electrifying if not dignifying, enough.

Plus, …I'm also, almost, certain; that, my mother's Seminole ancestors would be pleased, and proudly, of how she's kept her ancestry, alive, and, continually. Oftentimes, she's passed right along—to us, oral histories, mementos, and pictures of her…, or our ancestors…. Even, her very Indian-influenced mentality; emotionality; physicality; and, spirituality—all, are large parts of obtaining, retaining, and, maintaining her well-rounded—Indian identity. OH, MY! Does she balance it all, well, and, extremely, in some plain yet pretty and leathery or terra-cotta-colored pumps, shoes?

The powerfully perfect couple of a pretty powerful duo is still stepping steadily toward us, or Zara, Rex, and me. I'm sensing, too, that they're quite ready for our family brunch, which is now starting, officially, or, so to speak.

That, we're all now greeting or meeting each other, hugging, plus kissing one another, smilingly, and, lovingly, and even supportingly. That's right. For, the Zolden family, as a very sure rule, has supported each other's big bid to be something far bigger and far better than ever. Just, like my gustily go-getting bid; rightly, to acquire a new real estate, holding, right, for my real estate, division: A marvelously multi-family dwelling that's on the Palm Coast….

"All right now," speaks my father, Zack; "and, just, like it used to be said right in my Uncle Sam's Air Force," smiling, if not, smirking, some; "let's now chow down or now eat up," and, leading the way—right, to the circularly big and buffet-styled table; whose very circular contents are so delicious-looking: a very appealing appetizer, fruit-crab cock-tail, and tasty cock-tail sauce; some shrimp-rice soup; some honey-wheat muffins; some lemony salmon-steaks; some brown wild rice with mush-rooms and even buttery herb-butter; some cheese-frosted cauliflowers; a very fresh garden salad with some vinaigrette dressing; a very fruity fruit-medley salad; a pretty peach short-cake; some smooth chocolate-almond ice-cream; plus, for our simple drinking pleasure…: some very dry sherry; and, some very sparkling burgundy; and, even, some plain sun tea: Oooh, wee…!

I just murmur and then exclaim, "Hmmm, and what a fabulous feast of a sea-food brunch…, Mother!" moving, along.

"Oh, yes it is…," comments Zara, and circling the table, as well as gathering some food stuff; "but, do you've room for everything…?" she questions me.

"Yes, of course, I've room…," I tell her, "because I've since made room, right, on purpose, by having had just a snack, this morning. 'As, it's what I do…, most, typically, for Sundays' lunches or brunches,'" and gathering up just about every thing right from the buffet, table. My choice of dessert will come, later.

Pushing right back her lustrously long, blue-black, and super shiny hair behind her ears; that're bejeweled, and culturally, or ethically, with some Indian jewelry—or, some sizably turquoise-colored studs, ear-rings: "Not to worry…, Son," adds *Zakira*, "for some extra calories, or some extra pounds won't even hurt you. Because, of all the exercising that you do—"

Rex just interjects, or interpolates, "Before I forget, Bro," and, grinning, some-what, (still); "we've to set a real date to get together for a serious game of tennis—"

"That sounds good, 'or, damn good…!'" I respond, so rapidly, and roundly. Since, that'll be a damn good time to probe Rex's mind, or his peculiar rules and reasoning…, privately. What's really going on…, uh?

"All right…, everybody," states our big boss, or my father—Zack; "this fabulous food just needs to be blessed, first," and heading right to our circular table that's covered circularly.

It's been set, already, with a lacy-like table-cloth, a big beautiful bouquet of sun flowers, some shiny utensils, and all.

Before pouring her-self a small glass of dry sherry, *Zakira* asks me, "What're you drinking, my Darling Son?"

I reply, "Just some plain sun tea," and, not, wanting to mix things up, too, much. I'm just referring to my insides still digesting some poison…, or Chivas Regal. In fact, I'm feeling rather mellow or even laid back because of it. Like, nothing is going to shake up, or down, or even around, my deliciously dreamy day, or dream. Obviously, it's dressed, successfully, and, quite, with roundly romantic anticipation or expectation. Just, stay steady…!

"Okay," volunteers *Zakira*. She then pours the plain sun tea for me as well as wink at me, un-superficially.

Every one else has either gotten or is getting his or her food stuff…, and all. Afterwards, we all sit down at our round-table…, so to speak. Since, our big Sunday brunches aren't just about eating or dining but even conversing if not pondering some production…. That's correct. What would our Sunday lunches be without some talk of big business? I aim, also, to make it my business, in which my father will be convinced….

Now, every single person is seated…. Next, *Zakira* blesses the food stuff. Then, each person does just as Zack has since suggested or said: just, eat up, or chow down. I'm looking around, too, right, at this small group of a family. It's a good if not a great family, right, on the surface; well, except, for Rex, whose fantastic façade still worries me…, some. Not, to worry…, though, because in due time, I'll get right underneath such façade or front wall. Or, I'll ascertain what's certainly causing his over-cheerful-ness.

Just, smiling, or, grinning, or, even, smirking, away, Rex exclaims, "What a gorgeous day it is to be a Rayland or a Zolden…!"

Just, hearing that…, we all only chuckle, or chortle, and lightly, in the midst of dining or eating. Ha! Ha! Ha!

My dad or Zack just questions Rex, "Why you're so cheerful and all?"

"Well, despite the real estate or big business bust…, my business is holding right steady…," answers Rex. Is he exaggerating and overly?

With very sparkly and light-chestnut-brown-colored eyes, my mom, or *Zakira* remarks, enthusiastically, "That's great…!"

…Chopping up or cutting down such enthusiasm or even circular cheerfulness, my sister—or, Zara states, most, somberly: "I wish that I'd say the same thing about Zolden Enterprises' account-receivables…, and all, needless to say. Since, some folks are falling way behind—right, with their mortgages, rental payments, and all."

Very, soundly, super somberness seizes us and then squeezes reality—right, back, into our so-called, gorgeous, or delicious day.

Continuing, right, on, "I've been debating whether to use some funds from the company's contingency fund or its cash reserve fund—"

"…I've to suggest that the contingency fund is most appropriate, to use. Since, we want or need to hold on, and, tightly, to the company's cash…."

I only shake my head in absolute agreement.

Zack, just, continues, reminding us of an incredibly important fact…: "Please, remember, always, and, forever, that Cash is King and will remain so, for ever more," and then flavoring some of his food.

"…So very true, My Love…," *Zakira* agrees right with Zack amid savoring some of her food.

"Yes, indeed…," speaks Zara, before swallowing some of her plain sun tea. At least, she didn't have to think twice or even thrice about mixing up alcoholic beverages. I'm speaking about that Rum of hers…, earlier.

"Well Dad, I've to just say—that, often-times, while Cash remains King, his sensationally sassy Queen likes to keep things moving forward, 'or fast….'" Carrying on, "In other words this just isn't the time to just let an absolutely attractive property just get away…. Just, like, this multi-family dwelling—or, set of thoroughly trendy townhouses. That, I've had my eyes right on, lately." Without doubt, it's sometimes necessary, (to a certain extent), to move or just act fast….

Glowingly, and lovingly, and even supportingly, my mother concurs, circularly, with me: "So true, My Darling Son…," and then flavoring some of her dry sherry…; "You be sure, too, to e-mail us or bring back some pretty photos of that property while you're on the Palm Coast. Or, while you're at that big bachelor's pad of yours—"

"Ahhh, Mom," I gripe, just, a bit…; "it's my east-coast get-away—'or, one of my east-coast hide-aways—'"

"What ever you say, Son," *Zakira* interpolates with a little bitty wink and a nice-sized smile or grin of a smirk.

Given that…, we all just gurgle or giggle. Yet, I'm dead serious about expanding my branch or my division of Zolden Enterprises. I'm even dead serious about ending my singleness or aloneness; the last of which, is my big secret, still. LOOK OUT…! That's correct—or, right! Ms. Caren Colson ought to be right on the look out for something very serious…. HA! HA! HA! I smile, or grin, or even smirk— cackle, and circularly, within.

"Well, Son," Zack says to me, "of course, I support your ambitions. Still, always, remain very level-headed, or cautious, and circularly, concerning any new acquisitions."

"…For darn sure…!" Rex pops in his well-meaning message: "One can never be too damn careful or safe…."

Now, Zara adds her very own special say-so…: "All I can say is that you're so right…, Babe," agreeing with, if not acquiescing to her very bland bed-warmer of a husband, rather presumably.

I state, "Well, I so thank y'all for the support—'or, for the half-hearted encouragement, un-like my marvelous mother's whole-hearted support. That's, almost, always, on my side, and, quite solidly, no matter what….'"

Everybody is so finishing up, eating, or dining. But, not, before we digest some of those definitely delectable-looking deserts. Rising, I proclaim, "NOW, the chocolate-almond ice-cream is yelling out my name—ZENALD…!" and proceeding—right, to the table, buffet.

There, I'll just gather up some super sure sweetness; whose silky or sensuous if not sensual softness will be the ending or the very beginning of a super sensational sojourn; which, I just plan to grasp or clasp without doubt or fail…. That is, Ms. Caren Colson had better not fail me….

At present, the rest of the Zolden clan is joining me, here, at the big buffet, table.

"Hmmm…!" my father just murmurs well above his breath; "the pretty peach-short-cake is NOW yelling out my name—ZACK…!"

We all only laugh out in super sunny delight. We're just delighted by this deliciously delightful day of a brunch, lunch. It'll be ending, soon, yet, not, soon enough, for me. You see, that, I'm only too damn willing and ready to get away; or, to just get underway; or even, to just start a brand spanking new day…. HURRAY!

Part II

The Palm Coast, Florida
The Following Day, Monday

Zenald & Caren

Dearly beloved, I beseech you as strangers and pilgrims, abstain from fleshy lusts, which war against the soul:

1 Peter 2: 11

I'm hearing some super sad sounds or singing of a song. Then, I look up and see some blackish-gray-colored birds flying just below the grayish-black-colored sky on an overly over-cast day. The wet ground even looks slippery. Still, I slide—or, continue, right, on. Since, I'm not about to let some woefully wet weather soak my decidedly delicious dream of a day, or deed—up. That's right! For, I've waited too damn long to meet her—Ms. Right, so to speak.

I'm also almost certain that I look all right. Because first impressions are so very lasting, I'm dressed in my near Sunday best: A dark-charcoal-colored, so finely made, and modern-fitted jacket with a notch lapel, side vents, and 2 buttons; matchable pants made of 100 % light wool; whose slacks are pleated and lined perfectly to my knees; a silkily burgundy-colored shirt is underneath such; and, burgundy-colored, leather shoes are on my feet. MOVE IT!

I've made damn sure, too, to be clean-shaven. I've even had my silkily jet-black and low-cut hair on my head trimmed right to perfection. NO, SIRREE! I'm not about to let anything soak up or detract from my delicious dream of a deed. That is, the deed is to be pretty, presentable, indeed.

I'm now sliding right onward or speeding forward. Glancing at my platinum wrist-watch, its shine is blinding me, momentarily. The Palm Coast's Realtor's Conference begins at 9:00 a.m., or, in about 20 minutes, or, so. And, of course, punctuality means something, almost, always. As, I've learnt such, and, well.

Well, actually, my mother or *Zakira* insists upon it, total timeliness, without doubt or fail. She even gave me a small—or, a large piece of advice at our family lunch of a brunch, yesterday: Be weary or very weary of fast-talking, fast-moving, slow-talking, or slow-moving females....

And, right, out of the blackly dusty blue, I see her, most, believably. Or, so I believe…. Ms. Caren Colson is stepping right out of the Palm Coast Resort that's right on the very scenic boulevard…; which is hosting the realtors' conference…; whose conference hall, I once visited, some time ago. "HEY CAREN…!" I just holler out, yet, not loud enough, apparently. Since, she's moving right on, fast, and, most fashionably. Then, right, out of the damnably and the dustily black blue, a male seizes Caren's utterly un-divided attention.

In fact, they're now greeting or meeting and rather affectionately. The twosome is even hugging. Next, the tall, muscled, and very tannish-orange-colored man even kisses Caren. Perhaps, such wouldn't be so damn disturbing or, so distressing, if he weren't kissing her on or in the mouth…. Does he now taste her tongue…? Hmmm, or yum-yum…: OH, NO…! Something is wrong, and, so terribly, with this utterly un-propitious or utterly un-pretty picture. That, I'm now seeing with very wide-open eyes.

Now, they're moving onwards, and, slowly, to the conference? I'll be damned…! I mutter or mumble or even rumble—grumble, right, under my breath. Steady. Having halted dead in my tracks, I'm somewhat stunned by such…. Who is he? What're they to each other…? Where are they truly headed…? Why would the super slick-looking seizer and Caren kiss like that? And, when I meet Caren, should I inquire…? Of course, I've to question her…! I would be remiss, and roundly, if I fail to do so, correct?

…I'll be goddamned…! I utter—or, better yet, just, grumble, and am no longer shocked or stupefied; right, to the point of my being iced right up, down, and all around— frozen, fundamentally. But, instead, I muster enough sense and stamina to keep moving or sliding on…; yet, I'm doing so, right, in another direction; which is to say, that I'm now disappearing, and confusedly, or bewilderedly, if not, quite mystifyingly. I want and need answers to my questions…, needless, to say: DAMIT! Steady now! And, MOVE IT…!

DINNG!

DINNNG: Now, I'm hearing a fantastically familiar sound. It's quite un-like that very un-soulfully sad sound of some darkly un-soulful bird's singing…. But, instead, it's my alarm clock that's sounding right out for me to rise and shine on a shinily sunny day. Already, it has its fair or just share of decay, or rot. Such just happens to be my damn lot, today. Yet, I just lie back, right, on my satiny, king-sized, and comfortable bed. Since, the alarm clock's sound is so dying out. It was sounding out…, previously, or apparently.

And, WILD…! Was that some damned dream, or rather, nasty nightmare; in which, I saw Ms. Caren Colson, failing, and fantastically. That's right—or, correct…! She's since failed me—if only, in the super subconscious space of my mind, heart, and body, and even soul. Should I just let her go…?

Per, chance, her fantastic failure, or murky, or even muddy mis-deed has been in or on the cards—Tarot Cards, that is. I want and need, roundly, to have an objectively real Reading done…, for it's been a while. I wonder sometimes if my mother's or *Zakira's* periodical Readings are just too subjective of me…?

Now, veering my position…, I'm just trying to get more comfortable. But, that nakedly nightmarish dream is causing me to be un-comfortable, and utterly, or circularly. Is it an un-pretty precursor of an un-prettily un-propitious occurrence that'll occur? Huh?

It's been my personal experience that both dreams and nightmares come true: in one way, or another way, or even some other way; and, on some day, or another day, or even some other day. And, the only question is its timing; though, such timing often-times is in-fused right with the past and the present and even the future. For it's all relative and roundly.

...I just prop two of my fluffily four pillows—up..., under my head. It needs to be on the incline and not some goddamn decline. I neither want nor need a woman that'll hold me back or take me down; right, to a dark, deep, cold, and dirty, and even shaky ground, floundering, along. Just, like some deeply dark-olive-colored fool.... Since, I'm no goddamned foolish clown. That's so bound to be wound all around on a damnably dark bed of disloyalty or infidelity: GODDAMNIT! Coiling up, I'm not so comfortable, none, at all.

Still, I'm so pleased, having left Naples comfortably early, this morning. I got underway at the crack of dawn. After having crossed the lower, or the middle half of the sunny or shiny Sunshine State; I stopped for breakfast right at one of my favorite highway-hideaways of a restaurant. OH, BOY...! The fantastically flavorful-banana-nut and super syrupy pancakes; some sweetly countrified ham; egg-white-omelet; flavorsome-cinnamon-nut cereal; plus, some tastily hot herb tea, and all; so filled me right up with brand new strength or will power or even staying power: *personal power*.

Afterwards, I just drove onwards to my villa-styled get-away. It's a relatively new, out-of-the-way, 3-bedroom, and 2.5 bath, and even 2-car-garage, dwelling. That's very near the saltily greenish-blue-colored Atlantic Sea. That's decorated so modernly with leather, marble, and so forth. I confess, also, that I absolutely appreciate the finer things in life. And, why's that...? But, of course, it's because I most definitely deserve such. That is, I've almost always worked

42

my butt off or my ass off to the very naked bone or bones, as it were. For example, there have been times when I've been too damn busy to even use the rest room. As my task or job, at the time, allowed for no break, at all.

NO, SIRREE...! I've almost never been one to just take advantage of the gorgeously golden-Zolden—spoon; that has been put right into my mouth since my birth into this utterly un-charitable universe. But, instead, my success in life has been so earned or produced without doubt or fail. I also like to believe or even trust that such is absolutely analogous with my ethics, morality, and character, or spirit; none of which has ever been bargained for, or borrowed, or assumed, or bought, or sold, or even stolen...; but, instead, it's been earned, my character, and, productively. Likewise, I shall continue to earn or produce such moral make-up or spirit, character: Right, by not lowering my standard—or, certain standards, which are very important, so intrinsically, and inextricably, to my existence, or being.

Now, I'm stretching right out on my bed and trying to get more comfortable, still. Nor can I help thinking all about the comfortableness of that seemingly super squeeze of an embrace; belonging, noticeably, or observably, to that super sleek-looking seizer and Caren. For damn sure, I'll so question her about it, tomorrow; at which time, we'll meet each other. Or, we'll eye-ball one another in an effort to get to know each other, concertedly, or expectantly.

Where's her mind, heart, and body, and even soul, exactly...? In totality, or even, in partiality, does Caren's being belong to anyone or someone, else, already? Maybe, it's that super slimy-looking seizer.... Utterly un-able to get comfortable, I just sit up. Steady. I even get up, un-steadily, from my roundly rest-less bed of a so-called refuge.... That super sinister-looking seizer, interestingly, looked just like a damned....

Damn, her…! I just snarl, or gnarl, and grabbing my house robe that's on the nearby chaise. I then check out the time that's right on my platinum watch. It's just lying on the night stand, glimmering, glimmeringly. My alarm clock went off at 5:30 p.m., sharp, when my afternoon nap was over. And, I could sure use a little poisonous crutch to lean on for support, temporarily; or, use something, to help me get—right, through the fierily blackish-orange-colored fire; which is burning right up my desire to greet or even meet Ms. Caren Colson.

Yet, right now, I need to tidy up, some; then, have a bite to eat while I watch the evening news on television…; then, review some business documents…; then, pump some iron (or lift some weights)…; then, square my self away for a brand spanking new day…, tomorrow; then, I'll indulge, poisonously, a circularly crisp shot or two of Chivas Regal, as well as a few puffs of a costly cigar; then, I'll just rest so that I can be very well rested, right, for a pretty possible, or a male-eat-female, or even a producer-eat-female, fight.

That's so right. In either case, I may've to just fight; or, do battle, on the surface, per se, with Caren's probably un-principled philosophy of life, or her rules and reasoning; plus, the methodology by which it's so lived—her loose-kissing or pussy-footing life, quite obviously. Steady now!

I'm steadily getting about the business of life, and, living it according to my own damn theory, or reasoning, and rules. Produce…! Or, produce some pretty productive productivity, rather, productively, with persistent or pushy productiveness; whose production can never be enough…, ever. Such is just one of my life's mottos, of course.

The fantastic scene is familiar. Looking up, I fail to see any grayish-black-colored birds, flying; right, under the blackish-gray-colored sky of a dustily dark heaven, singing, sadly, or most un-soulfully. Heaven knows, that it's still an overly over-cast day—just, like, in that nasty nightmare of a damned dream…. Still, I continue, right, on…. I'm just treading my steps so very carefully on the very wet-looking and very slippery-feeling sidewalk, or ground.

POUND! Right quick, I turn and then look around. Now seeing that such sound is only the hard-wearing, or the heavy-duty noise of a construction-man's tool—nearby, I carry on very smartly. I'm even listening to my brain and my gut; both of which are just ordering me to maintain my steadiness in the darkly stark face of whatever is out there in the near or the far distance. Most, likely, something dark is out there waiting either patiently or impatiently. To shake right up, down, and, even, around, my characteristically, or my classically steady foundation of life: Like, that starkly damn dream of a nasty nightmare…, bad luck, or hard luck.

Indeed, I'd be a fantastic if not a fabulous fool, too, if I fail to heed it, or the nasty nightmare of a dream…. In the super shady dream, I was dressed very different. Now, I'm just wearing a black-colored, multi-stripe, and, slim-fitted suit. That's still crafted finely with some fine material and some fine thread. First impressions mean something—still. I check to see that the third button of my silkily rust-colored shirt that's underneath my jacket is all buttoned up. I do so, right, whilst I continue making my way—up, to the entrance of the Palm Coast Resort.

Just, like, in that dream or nasty nightmare, I glance or peek at the platinum watch that's on my wrist. And, it blinds me, momentarily. Again, it's nearing nine o'clock. However, I'm not about to be blinded, what so ever, by any fast-talker or even slow-mover; who'll try to talk me in to making a very bad move. NO, SIRREE…! It's not going to happen: No, damn way! I say again: NO, DAMN WAY…!

Coming to the few steps that lead to the entrance, I just continue or carry on…, smartly. That is, my steps are somewhat weighted, or measured, yet deliberate, and quite; right, in a pair of rust-colored, leather shoes. Incidentally, I've chosen to wear a black suit, quite, deliberately: to ward right off any and all negativity, blackness, or darkness, and the like. That's correct or, so right…! Such gives me a most meaningful measure of height or might; rightly, to almost always stand right—up, and fight, for what's so right in my sight; instead, of sliding back, down, or, around, or, even, from side to side, right, in fright.

Now, passing right around some very fashionable, and, even, some very un-fashionable folks, that're making their way into and out of the resort…; I'm moving onwards but not that much farther, mind you. Since, I'm just about there, at the entrance of the big, and brassy, and even bold-looking door, or doors, as it were.

…Having since moved right through the circularly capacious corridor, passage; I'm now moving right through the lobby; whose light lighting, soft furnishings—or, décor, and all are rather inviting…. Shades of pink, and lavender, and even lime, all abound; right, around the spacious plus subdued yet luxurious or very well appointed plus pretty pricey—lobby—quite feasibly.

…I just pass right by an attractive or an exceedingly exotic-looking female…: With lustrously long, or lengthy, and very thick, blue-black-colored hair; chiseled features;

dark-tangerine-colored skin; and shapely body; busty chest; elongated nails; plus, stylish attire with accessories, and all. Though, I wouldn't dare to make a pass at her…. No, thank you! Since, I'm not at all interested in any female with fake hair, or fake body-parts, and all. I say again: NO, THANK YOU…!

And, pretty please, let's just keep things real—if, at all, possible. Thanks! Needless to say, that I wouldn't dare be interested in Ms. Caren Colson, either, if she's about any sort of fakeness, at all; which, just has to include her loose-kissing and her pussy-footing, right, on the surface, or most seemingly.

Moving right along, I'm heading to the north-west side of the building, resort; where upon the conference hall is located. Or, at least, that's where it used to be…. When, I last visited such…. Reaching the widely open doors of the conference hall, I'm greeted by a crisply clad greeter; who wastes no time, either, greeting me with a papered badge of some kind: "Good morning, Sir," he just says to me—and, ushering right off two other people…; "and, how're you, on this very glorious, spring morning…? Also, you're a realtor or a broker—"

"Morning and I'm just fine…, 'or am well as can be expected…,' thank you," I answer right up; "both, for I'm a broker and a realtor, 'among other things….'"

"Very well…," speaks the greeter, and handing me that badge….

"Thanks," I reciprocate, accepting it, or the under-sized badge of paper. I then clamp it right onto my jacket's collar…, slantingly; "All right…," I say; "thanks again and have a good day—"

"…Why thank you…," the greeter tells me; "and, I thought that I recognized you…, Mr. Zenald Zack Zolden. I absolutely appreciate your informative article that's right in

Realty Plus, magazine, in which you talk about using *high-priced tax-liens* as a so-called form of an investment."

"Oh yes, and I so trust that you've found it helpful or the info—"

"Why yes, but, of course...," expresses the greeter, enthusiastically, "for I've since checked out such—"

"Very good for you.... Now, if you'll please excuse me—"

"Yes, of course, as the conference will be starting—soon—"

"...That it will...," I certainly concur, circularly, and then disappearing. Since, I'm not about to allow any one or any thing or even any place, to eat away, in any way, at my earliness, or promptness. For, it means something—still.

I've now re-appeared in the conference hall, whose big, bright, and beautiful room is full of people. OH, BOY! This hotel of a resort sure likes its pastel coloring...: aqua-blue, and olive-green, and even mellow-yellow, abound, all around: wall coloring, paintings, furniture, tiling, and all.

...Most people are just standing about, and greeting, or talking, or even net-working, and so on. Some are just sitting down, roundly, at the round-shaped tables. Where, cream-colored folders, and pencils and ink pens, and even small bottles of sparkly water are ready for consumption or use. Quite, conceivably, few are here—just, like me, for an ulterior motive.

That is, I'm now scanning or surveying the room, so in-conspicuously, from my gluey position. It's right next to a vacantly and a shadily sideward table.... I'm just looking for her. So, where's Ms. Caren Colson? At least, last night, she'd the common decency to confirm our greeting—if not, our meeting each other, today, via e-mail.

And, then, right, out of the circularly crystal-clear blue, I see her…, most, believably. Caren is speaking with some super slick-looking male. That's clothed casually in a beige-and-brown-colored slack set of some sort. For, damn sure, it appears or seems just like his type is all about loose kissing and pussy footing, outwardly. OH WILD, I screech, silently, and am taken aback. That's so correct! I'm taken right—back, to that nakedly nasty nightmare of a damnably dark dream…; in which, I saw Caren and some male….

…Is it he—or, the super sleek-looking Selzer of a seizer…? Unfortunately, I didn't see his face in the dream, or nightmare. Neither, did I even notice his clothing nor its coloring in the nightmare, or dream. Even so, the two now seem or appear to be over-friendly, or very touchy-feely—feely-touchy—and all, on the exterior…. GOOD…! Or, it's great that my earliness is affording me such a tantalizingly tall tell-tale of a vision, or view.

…OH, NO…! I shriek, and soundly, within, and am shocked, or stunned, somewhat, all over again. Yet, I ought not to be that surprised. Since, both dreams and nightmares, almost, always, come to pass, or come true, without doubt, or fail. Needless, to say, that she's failing me…, externally. However, I want and need to give Ms. Colson a real chance to explain things, and, exceedingly. Like, what's her actual aim concerning, or, better yet, so regarding me, or us, more, precisely?

Now, Caren and that super slimy-looking male with shiny hair, and tight clothes, and even heeled shoes, and all; both are dis-engaging, currently, from their circularly cold-blooded coziness, right, on the face of it. That's just, too, goddamn cozy, for me, whether portentous or not! Steady.

Neither am I just going to continue standing by, nor continue standing back right in the super shady blue, or, in absolute amazement…: GREAT! It's very good—that, that carroty-shaded male of a very loose-kisser and even pussy-footer has disappeared, else where. Or, that he's now some where else, and, saying, and even, doing, God only knows what, most imaginably.

"Hey Caren…!" I shout out, some-what. Now, she hears and sees me without a doubt, fail. I glance right at my wrist-watch, right, quick, and am not blinded…. Seeing that I've a little time to greet or meet Ms. Caren Colson—or, so produce; I just accelerate my steps or my moves, and rather productively, as it were. Steady now! As, no zig-zagging or see-sawing or even wig-wagging is allowed, ever.

Since, we're just about to greet or meet each other. Or, better, we're just about to come face to face with one another in an effort to get to know each other, finally. I'm also un-sure of, which side such greeting or meeting ought to reside on: the formal, or the in-formal? I'll just heed my mother's or *Zakira's* advice: When you're un-sure of what to do about something or another—then, just—do nothing.

Now, approaching me…, "Hi Zenald," says Caren, informally, and smiling from ear to ear: Great! At least, in person, she has a good-looking set of teeth; which, by the way, in my very strong opinion, is somewhat indicative of a person's status in life…; "I'm so glad that you've made it, here. And, you look super spiffy—"

"Hello, and thanks…," I manage to say, cautiously; "so yeah, I've made it—here, 'but, to what actual avail…, uh?'" Likewise, there'll be no loose-kissing, or even pussy-footing, nor any thing of the sort…; upon this momentous meeting of ours, not, right away, or, right now, anyway.

Now, urging me onwards, to a semi-secluded table, "Let's just have a seat here…, so that we can talk…, before the conference starts," Caren states, leading the way.

While en route…, she even informs me—that: "My co-workers and I've a reserved table, already, so I'll have to join them—"

I just interject, "No problem, 'or, no biggie…,'" and thinking better them—than, that super sinister-looking or super slick-looking seizer….

Within a minute or so, I assist Caren in sitting down at a vacant or an abandoned table set in the rear section of the conference hall. Or, better yet, we're away from folks' purposefully prying eyes and overly open ears.

After having assisted Caren into her seat, I'm now sitting right down; and, then, getting right to the crux of what's been gnawing at me, quite, greedily: "So, who's the guy 'or the seizer,' that you're talking to, 'so damn cozily, and all?'"

"That was just Seth Seizer—oh, so sorry. I meant to say, Selzer—Seth Selzer."

"Uh-huh."

"We go way back, right, to our old stomping ground at Naval Station Mayport, in Jacksonville."

"Oh?"

"Yeah, we both just used to work as managers at the NEX, or the Navy Exchange, before we decided to become full-time realtors, and all."

"Uh-huh."

"Of course, my family, and all, is still right there in Jacksonville, where my father has retired…, since. I only moved south or near St. Augustine and Daytona Beach, and all, because of the beautifully blooming, or the attractively active real estate market in the general area…." Carrying, right, on…, "BOOM! Now, it's all crashed and is burning right up…!"

51

"For 'damn' sure…," I comment, circularly, "which is one of the reasons why I'm here, 'to capitalize on such.'" I keep things moving forward or onward…: "So, were you and Seth 'or, the seizer' ever involved, romantically, 'or, most pointedly, sexually? And, please, keep it real or speak the stark-naked truth…!'" I inquire out-right because I just require the down-right truth….

"That was some time ago. However, over-time, he's wanted to get back together—"

"Oh?"

"Yeap, but, just, too much damage has been done."

"Oh?"

"Yeah, and I'm not about litigating any old issues— or, re-carrying any old baggage, not, at all."

"Uh-huh."

"By the way, or, incidentally, I've to just say—that, you look exactly like your photo. That you've posted, on-line, un-like folks that post fake or aged photos, and all."

I remark—then, question, "And, the same to you…. 'But, still, you're for real…?'"

"Yes, I too try to keep things real—"

"That's good! In fact, it's the only way—"

"I know, although the truth often pains, especially, when it's all about one's gains versus one's losses," states Caren, so interestingly, yet rather truthfully. She even looks a tad sad if not mad.

Gladly, I tell her…, "Cheer up," and then glimpse, on the sly, at my wrist-watch. Since, time is of the essence without doubt or, fail; or, it's just how it goes…: The highs and lows of seconds and then minutes then hours then days then weeks then months then years; all of which waits upon no one…, ever: "Well, people are beginning to sit down," I state, looking round about.

"Yeah, for it's just about that time," Caren tells me, looking around, too.

That once sad expression on her face is even gone. Per, chance, it's the mere thought or action of finance over romance that has cheered her up, since? Or, since, she just spoke of one's gains versus one's losses?

Continuing, right, on…, "I've to just say—that, I'm really looking forward to us just getting away, together, or getting away from society, work, and all. Look out Cayman Islands…!" Caren carries on, excitedly, if not, breathlessly: "You still want to go there…, to the scuba diving capital of the world, right?"

It's so very interesting that she would mention such. Especially, since, I'm not satisfied with the sure sound-ness or the very validity of Caren's raunchy romantic status…: Or, even, Caren's self-styled stance concerning that super sinister-looking seizer…, Selzer. Maybe, he's nothing more or less than a smooth, male romance-scammer; who's just scamming, so-called, smart, strong, and successful females. That damned scammer or shammer…!

Caren just interrupts my inner thought or thoughts: "Well? Do you still want to go…? So that we might really get to know each other or really indulge one another," she asks me, smilingly, or seductively, quite seemingly.

Responding…, un-avoidably, "We'll see," I utter or mutter or even mumble if not grumble, finally; "when the time's right," and eyeing her down and then up then down and up, again. I just want and need to see the totally truthful picture…. Or, rather, I've questions that need answering— still: DAMNIT!

"All right…," says Caren; "we can just talk about it—or, us, later—"

I interpose:

> That's a 'damn' good idea. Plus, we can even do so, at dinner, this evening. That is, if you care to join me for dinner at about eight; 'where upon I aim, absolutely, to just ascertain what precisely your main game is? Or, do you just plan to blame that seizer for your seemingly un-pretty pain? And, I doubt so seriously that it's in vain or doesn't make you wane. Do such, by the mere mention or even thought of his goddamn name! Just, the same, that I'll have dinner with you. Still, I can't and won't, at all, promise you—that, you won't be tamed—or even, maimed....'
> Well.

A very small slice of silence ensues.... Then, Caren answers up..., "Yes, of course, I'll love to have dinner with you, Zenald. And, right now, I had better go to my reserved table. Since, it's just about time for this conference to start, in earnest. I'm just one of the featured speakers..., that're scheduled to speak, shortly."

"That it is, time...," I comment, and standing, up. I even attempt to assist Caren from her seat, un-successfully. Since, she's standing up, already. Next, Caren just seems to want to peck or kiss me on my cheek..., right quick. Yet, I just brush it right off, right quick; instead, I just grab hold of her loose hand..., right quick, (as the other hand is just clutching her purse); "we'll talk, later," I utter or mutter or even murmur under my breath, right quick.

She remarks, "All right. Then, I'll just see you, right here, at the resort—or, hotel, where I'm staying."

After that, Caren disappears right into the midst of people that're sitting down, still, at their reserved tables…, most presumably.

On, the other hand, I'm now returning to that gluey position—right, next, to that vacantly and shadily sideward table. There, I'll sit or stay awhile, to scan the scene—or, to check out Ms. Caren Colson in action, conspicuously.

I've since sat down in that seat…, just, in a nick of time. Since, a medium-sized, apt-acting, and Asian-looking man has risen right to the low-level plat-form of a sizable stage. He's dressed so smartly in business attire: attired in a navy-blue and modern-fitted suit; whose pants are pleated to perfection; in addition, his crisply powder-blue-colored shirt is matching perfectly with its multi-stripe-colored tie, and leather kicks, or blue shoes. …There is a big difference between being well dressed and being very well dressed…. Or, again, first impressions almost always mean something.

…I've a good first impression of the first featured speaker, already; who's now adjusting some microphone of sort. Eventually, he speaks:

> Good morning Everyone, and I'm *Woo Wong*, or your Host and Planner for this exceedingly eventful event. Some of you may know, already, that I've been a resident, a broker, and a realtor—or a business owner, here, for several years…. Also, I've taken great pride through out the years in support-ing diversity, here. To have done so, in our little heavy-eyed town or city. It has given me such satisfaction…. But, I'm not at all

satisfied about the definitely devastative decline of our housing market. And, that's why we're all here: To not only net-work, but, also, to suggest some serious solutions: to our real estate problems. That're cursing or crushing and, most circularly, our general area. Or, up and down and all around the coast-line. From St. Augustine to Daytona Beach, we've to help each other or one another: To lift or raise this down-rightly devastative decline—up…, and way…!

Mr. *Wong* just carries on, rather, passionately, with his introduction or super serious speech some more.

Meantime, I just continue scanning the scene…. I'm interested, so particularly, in that super slick-looking seizer: or, more, to the point, his inter-action—demeanor, and all. His table is some ways from Caren's table and even mine. Interestingly, or, not surprisingly, but, quite naturally, he's sitting with two other attractive females. He even appears to be some-what touchy-feely or feely-touchy with them, as well. They're a pretty physical bunch, on the exterior.

By chance, you've known somebody or another that just has to reach out and touch you: Do so, while he or she talks to you…, and all? Per chance, it's a physically in-born form of communication for him or her…. No longer eyeing that damned seizer…, I just dismiss him from my view, or thoughts; yet, it'll remain skewed. Since, I'm now thinking about Ms. Colson; who's rising to speak, most seemingly, and quite presentably.

I guess that she too places some true value on first impressions…: or, in particular, being well dressed—if not, being very well dressed. Caren is clad conservatively, right, in a crimson-colored, light-tweed, and medium-length, and even well-fitting, or figure-hugging skirt-suit; whose long-sleeved blazer just showcases some absolutely antique-like buttons; interesting, enough, that the silver buckles right on her squarely sling-heeled pumps even look antiquated, and, very. Such shoes are complemented, further, by her shapely legs; whose coloring or hosiery is matching flawlessly with that super smart suit of hers.

More often than not, when dressing for success less is best; which is to say, that clothing accessories—or, such quantity ought not to over-shadow quality…, ever; which is why, quite, possibly, that Caren isn't wearing hardly any add-ons or added extras, except, for some small diamond-studded earrings; plus, a diamond-studded neck-lace; and, even, a diamond-studded—right-fingered ring, or set; all of which, only, adds even more class to the classiness of what I expect to be a circularly classy lady; who, always, shows much class and less ass—however, fantastically fine that it may very well be.

Her physical features are classic, even: With light-brown-colored skin; un-arched, yet well-shaped eye-brows; beautifully dark-brown-colored eyes; extensively thick eye-lashes; semi-pointed nose; glossily full lips shining just like starkly dark marcasites right under candle-light; plus, pretty plump cheeks; all of which, just, rounds out, so roundly, the absolute attractiveness of Caren's fine features.

But, such good looks, and all, can almost never be enough…, ever. Still, I thank goodness, that, at least, she's keeping some things real. Or, I so thank goodness that she's not about fake hair, or fake body-parts, and all. Her brightly brownish-black-colored hair is in a some-what sexy bob of some sort.

Right, beneath Caren's sexily conservative exterior, what is her true interior like, most truthfully...? Or, most, pointedly, is she just as brainy and gutsy...? That's right...! A foolish and feeble lady or woman is so value-less to me, romantically, and, very, without doubt, or fail. Hail right to all the wise and well-built woman of the world...! There's simply no time or place—or even, space, in my life for any un-called-for failure or failures, let-downs, as it were.

Quite, propitiously, Caren is not failing in her very strong presentation..., having since risen; and, having since introduced her-self; and, even, having since gotten right to the core of her utterly up-beat speech; in which, she's been speaking all about how realtors just have to be more openly benevolent concerning their real estate leads, listings, and all.

In essence, sharing, and sharing very generously is now the new norm, or the new name of the game-plan; or, even, realtors that're way down at their heels..., currently, must lift each other—up; right, by helping one another in every conceivable and allowable way. Do such, also, at the risk of sharing their un-propitiously prospective prosperity, or sure lack of wealth.

Fortunately, or, rather feasibly, I'm fairing so much better than most. For it has everything to do right with my hope, faith, and ambition, and even strength, or sure staying power: *personal power*. To just flower, pretty, powerfully, above all that would hold me back or take me down to the ground, floundering, about. Very, courageously, I just need to keep getting right through whatever is bad to get right to whatever is good, always, and, forever. Or, just, keep my commitment to and persevere in all of my circularly chief causes.

In fact, I'm just about to get underway, to conquer this romantically questionable day.... That can't and won't hamper my business or, a very chief cause of mine. This is to say, if I just can't and won't be successful, romantically, then, at least, I can and will be successful, professionally. Perhaps, it's the very best revenge of all: success, correct?

Without doubt, or fail, I'm now rising and shining, like the roundly reddish-orange-colored fire-ball.... It's just standing guard in the un-cloudily baby-blue-colored sky of a heaven. Since, I'm not about to be a fantastic failure or a big no-show. Or, don't show up at my scheduled business meeting of a circularly chief cause...; which will be soon or right after an early lunch, or brunch. Such would be a great big NO-NO, or a great big NO-GO. HO, HO, HO...! Once, more, I'm on the damn go.... Steady now.

...I wave good-bye or bye-bye at Ms. Caren Colson, on the sly—right, before I leave the scene.... HEAVE HO! Should I just let her go...? Huh? We'll meet or greet each other, later, and, much; where upon we'll so eye-ball one another; right, in a circularly colorful or an un-colorful yet concerted or even concentrated effort: to continue getting to know each other, better, and, much.

Part III

The Palm Coast Resort
Later That Evening

Zenald & Caren

Let thy fountain be blessed: and rejoice with the wife of thy youth.
Let her be as the loving hind and pleasant roe; let her breasts satisfy thee at all times; and be thou ravished always with her love.
And why wilt thou, my son, be ravished with a strange woman, and embrace the bosom of a stranger?

Proverbs 5: 18-20

…That, oh, so, roundly reddish-orange-colored fire-ball standing guard very high, right, in the uncloudily baby-blue-colored sky of a heaven is no more. …It's since turned right to a darkly brownish-red color. It's even falling very hard, on the blackly dusty-gray-colored horizon, under the dustily grayish-black-colored heaven of a sky.

Withstanding such…, the ambient temperature is so radiating, perfectly, 74-degrees, Fahrenheit. Or, so it seems to me. Though, the number 74 or 11 or even 2, when added, right, together, don't necessarily portent anything good or great, in balance. That's correct. For, I don't just study the science of dreams, but I even study the science of numbers, or numerology.

Speaking of numbers, ours is coming to pass—and, right here, in the present…. What about the future or our future, Caren's and mine…? That it's almost 8:00 p.m., on what I so hope will be an extremely eventful evening of a dinner, or date: OH, WILD…! How time just flies right by, disenchanting the foolishly gullible souls; that believe in its ability or its capacity to just bring good or great things—to pass: Flower! Or, bloom, in all its greatly golden glory.

Why couldn't it have been a glorious morning…, in which I didn't see that super sleek-looking seizer right with Caren? Huh? Yet again, I, or we ought not to be surprised by such…. Because, it's what that damn dream of a nasty nightmare has warned me of, right? With some luck, Caren may prove it—or, the nasty nightmare of a damn dream, to be wrong. In due time…; still, could it be on our side, time? I surmise as well as submit that only Father Fate or Mother Destiny knows such answer with complete certainty.

After having left the conference hall, this morning, I rode by the multi-family dwelling; which, I've intended to acquire without doubt or fail. For some time, I just sat there in its parking lot. I was checking out, or observing the flow of the traffic in the area, plus snapping a few photographs, and all. (I even e-mailed a few of the pictures right to my folks in Naples.) It's just smart to do so: Observe or check out a prospective property's flow of traffic…, and all, right, before its acquisition. Or, to just get an actual feel of what goes on…, actually.

After that, I headed back to my villa. Where, I got comfortable enough to exercise, some, in my in-house gym. Where, I just pumped or lifted some iron or weights. But, not, before I reviewed my business paper work.

Then, I just ate a deliciously light lunch or brunch; which, so filled me right up with spanking brand new hope, faith, and ambition, and even strength, or staying power— *personal power*; so rightly, to just flower pretty powerfully above any un-necessary negativity, or more accurately, any un-due doubt. Still, I've my damnably dark doubts….

It's only the highs and the lows of the blows. That, just, keeps blowing me right into a blackly grayish-blue sea of utter un-certainty. I'm certain, however, that, at least, my large bid for that multi-family dwelling—or, set of trendy town-homes just couldn't and wouldn't have been beaten. Especially, since, the reigning King is and has been right on my side, usually, and stably, or sturdily.

I'm just talking all about having paid cash, or three quarters of a million dollars—plus, right, for that real estate property; or, for that circularly chic complex…, during that pretty propitious, business meeting of mine. Its owner—or, past owner, that is, un-fortunately, is way down at his heels in down-right debt. Or, better yet, he's bleeding, and, quite, profusely, deeply red-colored dollar-signs.

I was even given a sign, previously, via a dazzlingly deep dream of mine; in which some man was all wound up and running all around town; just, like some damned down-and-out hound of a clown; that was bound, in-arguably, to failure—lest some seriously fast cash just pounded down—right, on him.

More, it was the super sure sound—or, the POUND of my pretty potent poison or circularly crisp Chivas Regal and costly cigar…: (an *Arturo Fuente Opus X "A"*); both of which were next in order—(but, only, upon my successful return…). Neither was any weight, nor a romantically un-certain fate of a weighty date going to weigh me down, to the damn ground, floundering, along; just, like a fabulously foolish fish in a starkly dark fish-tank so full of super salty nothings.

And, nothing is now going to stand in the way of my getting right to the very bottom of Ms. Caren Colson's seemingly sordid story of excusable explanations, and all; or, rather, her having tried to explain such solid see-sawing, or zig-zagging…, and all. Doesn't she realize, and roundly, that, there's absolutely no time or no space—place, for any goddamn wig-wagging…: or incompetence, and ignorance, and even stupidity…?

Luckily, and presently, I'm so utterly un-affected by those pretty poisonous pick-me-uppers…. In other words, I've planned…, carefully, and very: rightly, to be straight-headed, and heavy-handed, and even cold-blooded, among other things…; right, while I face Caren—down, and, way, down, to the damned ground if it's necessary. Steady.

It's also necessary that I get right ahead of the super sluggish car, which is moving, so, sluggishly, or too damn slow. GO…! Since, I've a particular place to be, something particular to un-cover, and someone in particular to meet, greet; whose greeting or meeting had better not disenchant me, not, a bit. MOVE IT…! This is to say, that I'm now moving forward or cruising onward with some speed.

Since, time or punctuality is almost, always, of the essence. Likewise, I'm just about there…, essentially. Yet, such could and would never be enough...; which is why, exactly, that I speed up, considerably, and, most noticeably. I'm now en route to the Palm Coast Resort: or, a heavenly huge hotel, on the outside, of course.

And, what should I expect to find, precisely, once, I'm inside or even on the outside of the hotel, or resort...? Without a doubt, I know that time will continue to tell the story, or our story, Caren's and mine. But, will it tell such story kindlier? I sure hope so. I've to just get my curiously anxious or my anxiously curious butt—there. Not, before I stop off or stop by a fantastically fine-looking floral shop, though. Steady now!

I've since parked right in the parking lot of the Palm Coast Resort. I'm now making my way toward the entrance of the resort, hotel. Or, I'm en route to see her, right, now. I trust, as well, that Caren Colson can and will appreciate the most beautiful bunch of flowers to be had, ever. Things had better work out for us—or, so I hope, still. Since, so much has been invested in our so-called, vested relationship, thus far: time, energy, and so on.

From the very first time that I so eyed Caren—right, on-line, I was taken right in by her and then later: or, ...by her outward politeness; kindness; generosity; and, sense of humor; and, even, self-respect—or, so I thought.... Having super self-respect or a super sensible sense of worth means something, indeed. Our subsequent mail, e-mails, web-cam photos, instant-messaging, telephone calls..., and all; plus, Caren's so-called desire to end her singleness..., and all; all of which had convinced me of her so-called sincerity. Now, I'm nearing the door of the hotel, or resort.

However, over time, I've so come to know..., and, very, well; that distance and absence or in-visibility can and does weave a starkly dark web of lies. I'm referring right to the kind of bald-faced—or, double-faced lies, that're just intended to impress, and entice, and even enmesh one. Such is why, so specifically, that I much prefer to meet a lady or a woman, romantically, up close and in person, first. So, I won't only know if there's any physical attraction but also I'll be able to read her. At the very least, I'll be able to read right in between her very short and even her very long lines of lies, or excuses, and explanations—all.

As it were, I'm now moving right through the door or doors of the hotel: GOOD…! Its lobby isn't as crowded, as earlier, or this morning. Still, some very fashionable and very un-fashionable folk with brief cases, baggage, and all, are just busting or hustling to and fro…. They're right on the go: ho-ho-ho!

OH, NO! I just shriek in down-right dis-belief. For, that roundly romantic scammer or shammer is right—here, on the scene. Or, better yet, I'm seeing the most believable sight of that super slimy-looking seizer. He has the absolute audacity, even, to have since changed clothing. He's now in a much tighter out-fit—or even get-up than earlier—or, this morning. Still, with greasy-looking hair, heeled-shoes, and all…; he looks just like the super sinister-looking romance-shammer or scammer; that, I've so judged him to be, down-rightly, or out-rightly.

And, why's that damned scammer or shammer here, anyway…? Having halted right—dead, in my tracks…, I'm being taken aback; right, to that damnably dark or nakedly nasty nightmare of a goddamned naked dream…. I'LL BE DAMNED! I squawk with very wide-open eyes and mouth agape, absolutely. Plus, I'm now motionless and speechless or frozen, fundamentally, right, by that super slimy-looking seizer.

Yet, I just manage to look around, looking to see if Caren will or will not appear—right, on the scene…. OH, NO…! I just manage to squeak right through the absolutely awful iciness of this super sour or super sick or even super sadistic scene, setting. Still, I'm so glad that I've shown up, so early, for this super bitter-sweet show-off of sort. And, of course, there has to be some type of show-down or face-off…: Right?

Now, I'm just seeing her walking slowly and then quickly—right, toward that super seizer… She's dressed so casually…. Once, again, their very un-mistakable greeting or meeting of an extreme or an excessive embrace is taking me way back, and, rather, un-propitiously. That's only too god-damn touchy-feely, or feely-touchy…, for me. …I'LL BE GODDAMNED! I just squall, so un-freezing my own damned self. Steady now!

…Dread and disenchantment or disappointment and even disgust—all are enveloping me; right, into a woefully wicked web of wickedly woeful wonderment…: or, super sure stupefaction. I'm not stupid…! Quite simply, I'm quite reasonably angered or mad and even sad. THAT'S RIGHT! …I'm just as angered as I can be…, and, quite, reasonably: GODDAMNIT…! I just bawl, especially, seeing the two or the twosome; whose embrace of an entanglement whether excessive or not, will never fail to ever elude, or delude, yet exclude me, most certainly.

Since, I now have seen, heard, smelt, and felt, and even tasted enough, already, of the sourly; if not, the saltily lip-smacking lies, or, even, the circularly crazy cries of so-called innocence. Innocently, I'm only standing by, even if, some-what, stealthily, or, on the god-damn sly…. Or, more, accurately, my circularly concrete conviction so concerning punctual-ness has permitted me such. I'm talking all about being clever or crafty when I want or need to be so. Again, should I just give Caren the goddamn heave-ho…? Or, just, let her go…? Then, turn right around and go…? Huh?

OH, NO! Now they're kissing good-bye? HELLO! I bark, being brought right back to my reality: The real-ness of my so-called date with fate or, with an utterly unseemly and fake mate; who, most probably, wishes that I'm late for such date. I've been some kind of very early bait—uh, to be used just like a pretty pricey rake; or, rather, to be raked right through a use-able, a mis-use-able, plus an abuse-able gate…?

Now, I'm only feeling a well-known ache that's just aching to be abated or vacated and not placated, at all. I say again: ENOUGH…! In other words, I'm done being polite, and all, right, to Ms. Caren Colson. In fact, she's just about to see—what, being pretty impolite, looks, smells, sounds, and feels, and even tastes like. Neither do I want to fight…, tonight. But, it's some-times necessary, and, very, to bite first or just fight with all one's goddamn might; so, rightly, to obtain, retain, and maintain some real sight and height or even might; right, above the goddamned female-eat-male—fight. That's right! Produce…!

NO, SIRREE…! I don't think that I'm just going to take flight like some fantastically flimsy kite of a damnably weak and foolish knight; who just tolerates being jabbed or stabbed in the back and then the heart with a jaggedly sharp butcher's knife. OH, HELL NO…! She's not about to mess up my life, not now, or ever…! I say again…: NEVER…! Steady.

Hence, I just intend to end what has yet to begin…, so truly. That is, right, upon super steady ground, I'm now moving on, finally, to the great big and round receptionist's desk. Since, that super slick-looking seizer and Caren both have parted ways, only partially, quite, presumably. Or, the two or twosome has since gone their seemingly separate ways, for the time being, anyhow. Still, I'm not about to be fooled, any damn more!

Because, I'm not some sort of super sweet sucker of a fool…, none, what so ever. That super slithery seizer of a shammer or scammer or even scoundrel just slithers, right, pass me on his way out of the resort, hotel. DAMN HIM…, I just bawl. Steady, now. Just, the same, that I want to hurl Caren's beautifully big bouquet of fabulously fine flowers at that slick; or, sleek; or, slimy; or even, sinister; and, sour; yet, sick; plus, un-stationary seizer of a damn scoundrel; or, a damned scammer; or, even, a goddamned shammer…!

…Instead of doing such…, I only offer him a very fantastically furious frown…, and fuming, mad. I'm getting damn tired, too, of just boiling over, or just boiling up, with reddish-black-colored—or blackish-red-colored blood…. In either case, please, stay with me. Since, I'm about finished with my damned tongue-twisting…. Or, better, we're about finished, here; where upon I've been trying—only, to bring one of my best dreams to reality; or, even, trying to end one of my worst nightmares, in actuality. Steady. Or, focus…!

Arriving at that big round receptionist's desk..., I'm greeted, and, promptly, by a short-sized, some-what stout, and even pale-faced female; whose pastel-shaded out-fit or uniform just isn't doing her complexion any favors. Just the same, that, she smiles rather brightly—or, cheerfully, prior to speaking: "Good evening, Sir, and how may I help you?"

"Good evening—and, I'm Zenald Zolden—here, to see Ms. Caren Colson."

"Please, just let me give her a call or a buzz, first," states the receptionist.

I just remark, "All right…," and watching her step aside.

Now, she's right to the side—or, right, in front of a computer terminal of sort. The receptionist is just checking out something or another concerning Caren…, presumably. Afterwards, she telephones her, or Caren's room…, quite, presumably. The two then exchange a few words. Next, I'm given permission to carry on.

Or, the receptionist tells me, stepping back in front of me, "Okay, Mr. Zolden, for Ms. Colson will see you in room—337. Oh, incidentally, I've to just say—that, you're surely carrying the loveliest roses that I have ever seen…! And, Ms. Caren Colson is a very lucky lady…, indeed," she adds, most, smilingly. So, ironically, the numbers 337 or 13 or even 4 aren't necessarily good numbers…. BOO, HOO!

…How very little that receptionist knows…. And, responding non-verbally, I only smile or smirk, outwardly; then, internally, I just frown, looking down and then up…. I'm even stepping away with long and heavy or deliberate steps…. Since, the weight of this so-called, romantic trip of mine is just weighing me down—though, not exactly, to the damn ground, yet.

"Have a lovely evening…!" the receptionist's raised voice trails me, roundly.

I just holler—back, over my shoulder without ever turning or looking around: "Thanks, and the same to you!"

Needless to say, that I doubt it seriously…; that, I'll have a lovely evening. In fact, it's a very fair assessment to just say, that, what's lovely is only one half of one of life's biggest dichotomies: plus, the other half is none other than what's so ugly; both of which, ugly, and, lovely, feed right off of each other while spew right out one another without doubt—or, fail.

Damit! I gripe, just, missing, the elevator that's now heading up. It'll be back down, soon, enough. At that time, I'll ride it right up to the third floor…, un-failingly. There, what's light may very well turn dark…; and, what's lovely may very well turn ugly…; and, what's right may very well turn wrong; and, what's good may very well turn bad. Such are only a few of life's big dichotomies.

…Two other people are just waiting for the elevator right alongside me, yet, not, as impatiently, quite probably. In other words, I'm through being patient…; or, my waiting for that—which, may never come to pass…. Because, I'm a rock-solid believer in destiny or fate: If something is meant to be—then, it'll be so, if not, then, it won't. That's correct, for I now believe that Caren and I both aren't meant to be, together, romantically, and obviously. Perhaps, we're never meant to be, together, romantically, and obviously.

Since, I've been so disappointed or disenchanted or even disillusioned and down-rightly, right, by time; and, by its so-called capacity or ability to bring good or even great things to pass, blossom! Or, flower, fantastically. However, I'm no fantastic fool, believing foolishly in a romantically foolish fairytale. That has yet to flower or flourish even a teensy-weensy bit, fundamentally. DAMN! Am I…?

The elevator has arrived and none too soon. Soon, time will continue to tell and then end our story, Caren's and mine. Once, more, will it tell such story kindly, hardly! After some people leave the elevator, the other two people and I enter it, elevator. We're now heading up…. I'll be the first one, too, to depart the elevator.

The elevator stops at the third floor. Then, its door opens up…. Next, I make haste not to waste any more time, fooling around with a seemingly shaky and shady or seedy

72

female; who, so apparently, doesn't have a goddamn clue about my real want or need to end what has yet to begin…, really. However, Caren is just about to find out…, truly.

"Good day," I just offer the two people that're left in the elevator. Since, I ought not to just cast aside common pleasantries, so completely. My having manners, (and good manners…, mind you), almost, always, means something, just, as regularity, or reliability, punctuality. Looking at my platinum watch, I just smile or smirk or even grin and then frown, with-in. Within a minute or so, I'll be at the door of room number—337, producing, and pretty productively.

I just knock, loudly, silencing any damned silence.

The door opens up and Caren greets me…. Oddly, enough, she's now garbed rather prettily (or sexily) in pure or pristine white. It's the very color that roundly represents purity or piety…. Although, we know—by now, that Caren isn't at all pious, on the surface.

Just, wearing a short, silky, and sexy house-robe…, she sputters, smilingly: "Zenald, hey—you're so early. OH MY!" shuffling back, hurriedly, in a pair of white, feathery, and heeled house shoes. Such shoes could've been bought or ordered, easily, from the roundly racy magazine; which is entitled *Frederick's of Hollywood.* "And, don't you look so very nice—or, all spiffy," Caren compliments me—but, to what damn avail, uh?

Lateness, almost, always, has a very high price just as earliness…. I'm dressed down to a great extent, wearing only a black-and-white-colored, and retro-styled, yet well-preserved Nik-Nik shirt; plus, a pair of pants that're pleated pretty perfectly; whose bottom hems are flared, some-what, over my black-and-white-colored, leather shoes. It just pays to be old-fashioned…, some-times.

"OH WILD…!" exclaims Caren…; "What beautiful flowers that you've for me. And, please, come right on—in. I've to get a vase…."

I'm stepping right into Caren's hotel room, on the outside; yet, inside, I'm really stepping else where…: Just, maybe, it's some where else that's likened right to an un-pretty, pastel-colored bull-ring. Where, a typical non-bully may've to just bull-doze a fantastically foxy female, that's full of damnably dark bull-shit!

I shut the door and then get right into the male-eat-female fight of an un-typical bull-ring…. It's my intention, still, to get knee-deep or down and dirty while I'm in such bull-ring or clash, so to speak. PRODUCE…!

Accelerating right to the telephone that's on a desk, Caren states, and, some-what, excitedly: "OH MY…! I've to just get a vase for my gorgeous bouquet of flowers. I'm going to call house-keeping…!"

Before I respond or re-act, I just look around the room or suite, right, quick. Seeing a very nice-sized living room, dinette, and all, I just decide that none of it is of any damn consequence: Not even the prettily pastel-shaded, and absolutely abstract paintings right on the wall; or, the very lush carpeting; or, even, some super scented scent or smell; none of which is of any goddamn consequence…!

Subsequently, I speak, yet un-invitingly, or very un-welcomingly, more than likely: "Don't bother…! 'Or, most particularly, just, don't waste my precious time…,'" I scoff, sourly, or saltily, and strutting right to the trash can. That's near a partition or a divider of some type.

And, Caren even sees me doing so—"What do you mean…?" she asks me, ignorantly. Or, quite possibly, she's just dumb-founded—"Where—what—ZENALD—" Caren splutters, and senselessly: "Why you're putting—or, doing that?" she questions me, again, and rather inquiringly.

I just dump the prettiest of pink roses that I've ever seen—right, into the trash can, or the garbage can. Because, I'm not about to just give or present such flowers to her: or, light-brown-colored garbage, or trash, on the exterior. After having done away with the flowers, I'm now turning right back—only, to face her, or Ms. Caren Colson, right, down, to the goddamned ground.

She's just slings the phone—down, and hard, on its receiver: "What's your problem?" she inquires with widely bright eyes, and a widely open mouth—or, in super salty shock. Is she now beginning to see the light and what's so right? Huh? If so, it doesn't matter at this point in time, this evening, or tonight. Since, there still may be a damn fight, right, in sight, in which I shall take the very first goddamn bite. OUCH! For, it's going to hurt or ache just as it should, without doubt, or fail: HA, HA, HA!

…I just answer up—or back, slowly, then—in a big hurry: "Why're you running so late, and all? Or, better yet, what've you been up to, uh? 'And, please, or pretty please, keep it real…!'" I enquire—then, demand, eagle-eyed, and, extremely.

Slowly, she searches for something to say, "Ahh—hum, well, I'd to take care of this personal matter—"

"ENOUGH…!" I explode, explosively, or coldly, or even cold-bloodedly…; "Since, I've heard quite enough of your definitely dubious explanations, excuses, and lies—"

"What're you talking about?"

"You, Ms. Colson are a habitual liar and a habitual cheater, 'and God only knows what else…!' I saw you and the 'super slick or sleek or even slimy and sinister-looking' seizer—or, Mister Selzer, 'of a roundly romantic romance-scammer or damned shammer,' in the lobby—right, before I came here, to your room."

Just, signing in super subdued or super sour or even super salty shock, and, shaking her head, quite, slantingly; Caren is searching, once, again, for something to say, "I'm just trying to keep Seth out of our mix, or our relationship. That, I thought was flowering or blossoming and prettily or nicely," she purports, or professes, yet deludingly.

I just retort and refute or rebut and rebuff and even rebuke or repel Caren and roundly: "Why would you do or even think that…? When, 'I know, in fact—that,' you seem to be very much into bigamous, or, polygamous, or, even, promiscuous relationships…, and all—'but, NOT, Zenald Z. Zolden. Since, I neither want nor need any damn part of such damnably dark or dirty debauchery...!' Huh...?" Right, now, absolute anger is setting right in…!

…So voiceless, and motionless, Caren just listens as I carry on, angrily, if not brutally: "We're done or finished! Because, I now see or view you, quite simply, as an utterly unscrupulous, and a super scandalous liability, who, at the end of the day, will only hold me back or take me down! Un-rightly, right, down, to a starkly or a nakedly or even a damnably dark ground, just, floundering, so foolishly, if not fantastically! Or, even, stab or jab me right in the back and then the heart…! NO THANK YOU, 'Ms. Big Burden…!'" I spat, rather un-kindly, and seething, mad. STEADY! And, no more god-damn see-sawing or even zig-zagging—wig-wagging...! FOCUS!

Right now, she's well alive…! Motioning her hands in some fancy way and even voicing some harsh words…: "HOW DARE YOU!" Caren re-acts, finally, and slapping me with all her damn might—"SLAP!"

OUCH! I squeak, yet silently.

She continues with fierily blackish-orange-colored fire, burning, so fiercely, in her eyes, or being, most likely: "…You needn't patronize, or analyze, or criticize, or even ostracize me…, EVER! Since, I'm just trying to do what's right—"

"YOU'RE DEAD WRONG...! Or, you're deluding your-self, and, down-rightly, if you think, yet again, that I ever intend to put my hope, faith, or trust, 'and heart,' right, in you, and then just leave it there"; carrying right on, quite contemptuously: "to be so trampled over—or rather, to be butchered right up, down, and all around with a starkly or a sharply jagged butcher's knife. NEVER—EVER…! Since, the damnably dark damage has been done, already!" I scold Caren, scathingly, and scowling.

Gloweringly, Caren just slaps me on my face, again, with all her damn might, "SMACK!"

Of course, I intend to defend my-self—or, position, and, out-rightly, right, in the female-eat-male, bull-ring. So, I just battle right on! Or, I snap or crack, rather, scornfully, "WHACK!" delivering my own god-damn blow—right, to her that's both high and low…. And, NO SIRREE! I'm not exactly on the damn go…, just, yet! Though, Caren is more than likely just about to give me the god-damn heave-ho.

Since, I grab hold of her hand…, immediately, and tightly, just, as she's about to strike me…, yet again. "'OH NO!' DON'T YOU DARE DO IT…!" I go off or blow up, most, expressively, with fierily blackish-red-colored blood and fire burning my insides—right, up! "Don't even think about lifting another one of your fucking filthy fingers, to hit me…, AGAIN! If so, I so promise you—that, you'll be more than just slapped right back—but, instead, you'll be knocked right out—COLD, 'or, cold-bloodedly!'" I snarl, grimacing, grotesquely. STEADY NOW…! Since, absolute anger has well set in…!

Quickly, she retreats and then shrieks, so soundly, "YOU BIG BOORISH BASTARD! Just, get the hell out of my room! And, don't let the damn door touch you on your goddamn way out!"

…Before I back off or back away or even get out of the bull-ring, angrily, I just stare down this very backward liar of a circular cheater; who, I've since placed right into her place; whose pretty proper place or, super stifling space garners such or much mold—decay, or rot. Neither should I try to hold on, tightly, nor boldly; un-rightly, to somebody that's rolling, so roundly, if not duplicitously, in damnably dark debauchery, or even duplicity. That damned dis-loyal debaucher! I gnarl, gnashing my teeth, very angrily.

So fuming, and frowning, "I SAID—GET OUT—NOW, YOU, omniscient, omnipotent, and, arrogant, and even condescending—or, cash-grabbing ass—BASTARD!" Caren squawks, yet, again, and, backing up, fast. Because, she knows what's best for her…. Yet, it's too damn little and too damn late…! Still, is she now aching or breaking into some utterly un-pretty pieces…? I sure hope so—HA!

Satisfied, squarely, that I have since stood my damn ground, and roundly; I scoff, so soundly: "FINE! Since, it's high time…! Or, I don't care, any longer, to see you lie or whine, any further."Continuing, quite, scathingly; "Though, before I go, I've to just tell you—that, you ought to reflect, and roundly, or very seriously, on something. What sort of twisted, or perverted, or even sick female are you, beyond doubt? HUH?" Carrying on, and, rather contemptuously…: "By the way, or incidentally, you're just going to end up a nakedly old woman, and, ALONE…! Now, GODDAMN, GOOD RIDDANCE! 'YOU, GODDAMNED LOSER…!'" backing off, or backing away, and then turning around—producing, so productively, or propitiously.

Most naturally, Caren is now staring me right down to the ground, floor. She's even speech-less, and stationary, or just stock-still, all, right, to no god-damn avail…. HA-HA! God-damned super silly, super stupid, or super sick—BITCH, of a darkly damned female: or, LOSER, and MIS-USER, and even ABUSER…!

YES, SIRREE…! Or, YIPPEE…! I'm now on the damn go, having been given—since, the most hospitable—HEAVE-HO: Ho, ho, ho…! Back, out, up, and away, I now go…: HO-HO-HO! And, HA-HA-HA…! Oh, thank you! I so thank you, Father Fate, or Mother Destiny...! Plus, I just plan to keep things moving right forward, or onward, if not upward, as always. FOCUS NOW, and steadily…!

Part IV

The Following Day
Wednesday

Zenald

I say therefore to the unmarried and widows: It is good for
them if they abide even as I.
But if they cannot contain themselves, let them marry; for it
is better to marry than to burn.

1 Corinthians 7: 8-9

So, I've since left that scene or sleepy-eyed *setting*, right, behind, and, way. I'm even cruising, westerly, with considerable speed along Interstate-4, (or I-4). I look up at the review mirror of my pitch-black-colored *BMW*. I'm just looking at the starkly dark distance, which I'm putting amid the Palm Coast, Caren, and me—still. Enough, or, focus…!

…I return my very vigilant eyes right upon the road that I'm traveling on…. Since, I left my villa, this morning, after the break of day. As I'd to just get underway or just get away. Leaning, sideways, I'm reaching for the costly, if not the poisonously thick stick that's just smoldering in the ash tray. I thus flavor a lengthy draw of it. Then, I lower the windows of my ride even lower. My other poisonous love or pretty potent pick-me-upper will come, later, and, much.

There's nothing like flagrantly fresh air clearing my mind of all cloudily dark thoughts…. Plus, there's nothing like seeing things, places, and people just as they are; and, not, just, how I want or need such to appear or look. Hence, I take off my dark-shaded or rosy-shaded or even flowery-shaded sun-glasses. I do such, to keep every thing as real as can be, on the surface, at the very least. Focus, now.

…Multi-colored sun-rays get right in my way. Still, I'm not about to put back on my sun-glasses, just, yet. But, instead, I just continue cruising, effortlessly, with the help of my car's cruise-control…; cruising, right, under the very big yellowish-orange fire-ball that's still rising, right, in the absolutely azurean sky; right, on a goldenly gorgeous and spring day. HOORAY! As, I aim, too, to get rid of some if not all of its inevitable decay or rot, some doggone way.

I savor another lengthy draw of my poison and am totally thankful for, or pretty pleased by, my successful, business trip. My father and my mother both—or, the entire family, and all, are even pleased by, or very thankful for the pretty photogenic—if not, the pretty pictorial photos; that,

I've since e-mailed them of my new real estate, acquisition: or, the 132-unit, well-appointed, and multi-family complex of a hard-hit or a recession-hit, property.

Ha…! I smile or grin or even smirk, right, within…. I'm just smitten by my absolute capacity or ability to have made a roundly rosy-shaded dream of mine come so true: Flower! Or, bud in all its goldenly bright beauty, or glory. Now, I'm frowning, or even scowling, and disappointingly, or down-rightly: Because, Caren Colsen isn't the woman of my most delicious dream…; but, instead, she's just another doggonedly dark player in my roundly romantic nightmare.

And, to think, that I'd taken to her my widely open heart and the loveliest of flowers or pretty pink roses…. It's so good, too! That I've so heeded my mother's wonderfully wise words of a warning concerning the female-eat-male—fight. That's so right or correct…: Be weary or very weary of fast-talking or fast-moving or even slow-talking or slow-moving females….

BRAVO! Since, I've done well, professionally, and exceptionally, on the one hand…; right, on the other hand, I've failed, so personally, or romantically, and fantastically: rightly, to bring one of my most treasured dreams to reality or actuality. Boo, hoo! Actually, or truthfully, I'm far better off—not, having a woman as opposed to having one that is quite simply no doggoned good. Right, Fellows…?

…Any real man, whether white, black, or brown, or even tan ought to just understand such super solid stance…. Romantically, what's the real point of having such woman; who, at the end of the day, is all about super sub-standard-ness…; whose sub-standards or even sub-standard world is where she lives, works, and plays, in, uh? Yet, whose super sub-standards will never be suitable for the world, in which I live, work, and play, in. Never—I say again: NEVER…!

I go ahead and kill my poison before it kills me. Nor can I help just looking up at the review mirror, again. The doggonedly dark distance is widening and it's just as well. Or, never mind that I've since failed, and, miserably. Still, I'm cruising on, or about, and holding on, so tightly, to my decidedly delicious dream, rather romantically. HA! Since, I'm not about to let some hard-hit area; or, some hard-of-hearing; and hard-pressed; or even un-sound—and illogical female—just, squash my good spirits…. No, doggone way! I say again: NO, DOGGONE WAY…!

And, OH—BOY…! The would-be, up-and-coming Palm Coast has yet to be crushed, circularly, or fully. For, its real estate market will take one of the deepest dives of any metropolitan area. Plus, its employment rate will climb as high as any metropolitan area. That's right. These aren't just utterly un-pretty premonitions…. But, instead, they're realities, (or actualities), blooming, most gloomily, right, on the starkly dark and very brittle horizon; which, I've since capitalized on, quite calculatingly. Ha-Ha!

It's just GREAT! That, my darkly dichotomous date with fate hasn't been without some type of win…, to boot. Still, in the end, I'm single, and, solidly: DOGGONIT…! I bark, being brought right back, to the actuality or the reality of my singleness—or, aloneness. Although this isn't to say, that I don't appreciate, absolutely, the fantastically fine line between being alone and being lonely. Because, the two—alone, and, lonely—just, pose two very different scenarios, or situations.

Just, the same that I truly don't want to find myself lonely or even alone at the age of 45—or, in 5 more years, more, accurately. Plus, what 40-year-old woman so chooses promiscuity, right, over fidelity and most illogically? Huh? The absolute answer is Caren Colson. That doggoned loose kissing and pussy footing female of a very fantastic fake or doggone ache!

Well, as least, most of the mature or aged people that inhabit the Palm Coast, so fortunately, are well hinged in faithful relationships, marriages, and all; which may very well be a factual testament of age, experience, wisdom, and the like. Rather, interestingly, *Mister Woo Wong*, or, that Asian speaker and business owner spoke honestly about the Palm Coast's quest; or, its struggle, as it were, to diversify its population. So true, too, that, there are hardly any or no minorities in that sleepy-eyed area of the Atlantic Coast.

Granted, that's all now changing, especially, as outsiders from round about move right in. To capitalize right on the fantastically fragile real estate market of the Palm Coast. I just chuckle, or chortle, or even laugh, inside, and am too doggone glad that I've my-self done so, since. And, what about Naples, Florida...? It also needs to diversify its population.... But, most importantly, and speedily, it needs to get itself right off of the U.S. Justice Department's list of discriminators. That discriminates, so, discriminately, right, against voters, and, in particular, Hispanic voters....

I'm just capitalizing on the early, light, and, almost non-existent traffic.... I even glimpse at the platinum watch that's on my right wrist. Seeing that it's nearing 8:00 a.m., I just continue cruising with considerable speed. Or, I'm still putting some starkly dark distance very far behind me, so to speak. Since, home is where I'm now headed..., and, quite, eagerly. Steady now.

At this junction or juncture, my central *point of view* (or *P.O.V.*), is all about carrying on, smartly, strongly, and, successfully; while, at the same time, my being rather real. I just smile, or, smirk, or even, grin, right, with-in. Since, I now realize that my brother-in-law—or, Mr. Rex Rayland is most comparable to Caren Colson: That, the two possess such fantastic fakeness; which certainly comes from trying to be something or even somebody that they aren't, purely, and simply. Rex is a Zolden, want-to-be, while Caren is a player, want-to-be. Let's just forget about the two want-to-be's; both of whom are wanting and quite woefully or most doggonedly. Damn, the damned wanna-bees...!

Still, I've deduced such because of their mentalities and personalities or physicalities. Or, better, the absolute affectedness in which the two, or Caren and Rex both just present them-selves as up-standing individuals—or, down-right do-gooders: wanting to do nothing but good.... Haw! WRONG...! Plus, it's so bad if not sad that the two seem to be utterly un-aware of their own reduction of a super sick seduction.

GOOD! That, Caren didn't seduce me with her slick or sleek or slimy or even super sinister seduction: or, her great big box of lies, excuses, explanations, and all. Since, she has failed..., and, so fantastically, but, not Zenald, and, not, today, anyway. Since, today is a brand spanking new day; in which, I still plan to be a conqueror, and, not, some doggone conqueree; who's being conquered, and circularly, by some doggonedly dark forces or powers. Steady.

That's correct! I'll be doggoned if I permit the Palm Coast, Caren, or Rex, or even anybody or anything to hold me back; or, just, take me down to the ground, dithering, so dreadfully. In fact, ...I've a fantastic feeling...! That things are looking up—still, while looking down, all around, and all, even, if dichotomously. Yet, there's positively nothing dichotomous about my outlook on life: Ha-Ha-Ha!

In other words, I'm not about two minds or three minds or even more. But, instead, my one-track mind is just as before, moving forward, or onward, or even upward...: professionally, and, personally, if not, romantically. I've to just keep trying to find the lady or the woman of my most delicious dream. Or, just, keep getting right through what's bad to get right to what's good—or, GREAT! Most likely, that she's out there, or some where, in the beautifully bright distance: just, waiting, and waiting, for me, so expectantly. Haw-Haw!

Until we greet each other or meet one another, I'll just put my faith or my trust right in my delicious dreams, or high hopes. Yet, meanwhile, I've to just deal with one of life's biggest heart-breaks: heart-ache. That, Father Fate, or Mother Destiny has bestowed upon me…, since. It can and does cause such anguish; which, some-times, if not often-times, leads straight to an absolute argument of some kind: or, a circularly colorful *conflict* of some sort.

That, either Mother Destiny or Father Fate has seen fit, to bestow upon me such a circularly cold-blooded clash: Or, one or the other has so plotted that fate or destiny and I collide, coldly, or, cruelly. I'm not altogether sure of such answer, just, yet; which one…? Since, fate or destiny and its affect if not effect upon me or my life, almost, always, is of super sure significance; whose un-failing consequence—that, I, almost, never, am un-able to affect, nor effect….

Still, my oppositional *plot* or plan is to just carry on, smartly, strongly, and, successfully, without doubt, or fail. That's right! As, I'm not about to let my utterly un-naked date with destiny or fate just vacate my hope, or faith, and ambition, and, even, strength—or, staying power: *personal power*. Rightly, to just flower pretty powerfully above all that ever dreams of holding me back or taking me down…; right, to a nakedly, or, a starkly dark, deep, and, dirty, and even, shaky, or deathly ground, dithering, rather dreadfully.

This is why, so exactly, that I'm now speeding right up; so rightly, to get and then stay right ahead of the black powers or forces that be; which are posed, purposely, to do me in, and, perhaps, expertly. They're black or dark forces or even powers just like Caren's explanations, excuses, and lies…; which, so impelled, if not propelled me, to refute or rebut and rebuff and even rebuke or just repel such, or her, altogether. DOGGONE LOSER!

YES, SIRREE…! I had quite enough of that cold-bloodedly clamorous conflict of a roundly racy—or, even, a terribly tainted love-triangle; whose very loose-kissing, and very pussy-footing context equaled its pretty promiscuous, or polygamous, or even bigamous content; both of which—content, and context—I neither wanted nor needed any part of, and, none, what so ever. No, Sirree…! I say again: NO, SIRREE…! Steady now.

Needless, to say, too, that I'm even more than just conflicted about on-line dating…: or, more precisely, its so-called, romantic highs, lows, and blows; which, just, keeps blowing me right into a doggonedly dark—or, a woefully wicked web of down-right dis-enchantment: or, even, dis-illusionment. DOGGONIT, I snap and very angrily. That's right—or, so correct! I'm angered all over again. Steady!

There's something that'll help, surely, to maintain my steadiness while on the go—or, on the road…: a pretty poisonous smoke. Thus, I fire it or what's left of it…, right up. Next, I just flavor and then savor its sweetly poisonous might—or, sight, sound, smell, and feel, and even taste…; tasting, right, as its poisonously sweet poison just abate my down-right dis-satisfaction and irritation or anger.

Though, I just can't help thinking about the *climax* that's led—since, to my anguish and its absolute after-taste or absolute after-math. That's so correct. Mother Fate has plotted, also, that my conflict with Caren reached some sort of climax…. And, of course, it'd to just happen sooner or later. Since, such has been on or in the cards—Tarot Cards, that is, more than likely. But, first, we needed to see-saw, or, zig-zag, or, even, wig-wag, all about; right, in a roundly rigorous, if not, a roundly rebellious effort, to get right to what's real and bad and even sad. BOO, HOO!

Naturally, I'm rather mad. Since, I've to now start all over from "scratch one." In my quest to greet or meet a spanking brand new, eligible, and mellow-talking, and even mellow-moving female: or, a wildly wonderful woman of a very lovely lady; who won't jab—or, stab me—right, in the back or even the heart, ever, with a jaggedly sharp and big black butcher's knife. Or, even, fill my life right with any doggone dark strife. Still, I ought to be pleased, some-what. That, at least, I'll get right over or get right through Caren's very short-lived knife-attacks or even super sick stabbings. DOGGONIT, I squall, in doggone pain, just the same.

After all, I've since wasted my pretty precious time, fooling right around with a female of a seemingly fantastic fool. That, things have since dissolved, romantically, right, into a doggonedly dark state of dissolution, on the exterior. Yet, I've had to be resolute, and, roundly; right, in my out-right or even my down-right discharge or even dismissal of Caren's explanations, excuses, and lies, or her, altogether, and, forever! NO, SIRREE…! I'm not about to allow any female clown that's of two or three minds, waste my time, EVER!

POUND, for it's just the doggoned sad sound of an absolutely atypical ache. It wants to rape me, ravenously, or rather, un-romantically, of my deliciously good dream…: NEVER…! Since, I mean to hold on, quite tightly, to such; which gives me constant hope, or faith, and ambition, and even strength, or, staying power—*personal power*: rightly, to just flower pretty powerfully: BLOOM…! Or, blossom, most romantically. Steady now…! Some very warm or hot solids will help, too, to foster and then bolster such strength or power, steadily; which is very much needed, still, for the female-eat-male—fight, or struggle, as it were.

Thus, I just decide to stop at one of my very favorite highway, restaurants. Right, where, I'll have a solidly good breakfast. I'm now peeking at the platinum watch that's on my right wrist, again. Neither am I blind, nor being blinded by time that seems to be on my side, right, now. But, can it stop the poison from poisoning or killing me…? Huh? I go right ahead and kill my poison before it kills me, dead. Or, before, that zillion-dollar question is ever answered.

A car swerves right—dead, in front of me, changing lanes. HONK! I blow or sound the horn of my ride as well as shriek, soundly: DOGGONED JERK…! Steady now…! The point of my early travel isn't only to beat the rat race; but, also, it's to avoid, absolutely, the doggone likes of such ratty, or, batty drivers. I reach for my very dark-shaded, or rosy-shaded, or even, flowery-shaded sun-glasses. They're right near my cup holder. Then, I put them on with much or such pleasure. Because, I'm now seeing things, places, and people just as they are.

I'm seeing, hearing, feeling, and touching, and even tasting, right, in my mind, heart, and body, and even spirit; just, how my roundly raucous, or even my roundly riotous *resolution* concerning Caren has been plotted, un-prettily, or quite unkindly, yet necessarily. Or rather, how else could or would such a fantastically fervent fight, or an utterly un-lovable love-triangle take form or shape…, uh? Of course, I would've liked for the utterly un-fashionable shape or form of such solution or resolution to end more kindly. However, it just wasn't meant to be. Or, so it seems to me, at least.

Still, I'm some-what sad and mad and even glad…. Since, I just stood my dog-gone ground with that seemingly loose-kissing and pussy-footing female; or, that un-ethical, im-moral, and character-less female; or, even, that female, who's just so dog-goned character-plagued. Most certainly, she's just not marriage-material, at all, among other things.

Likewise, I trust that my failure to have enshrined Caren—or even, to be ensnared right by her, isn't a Shakespearean tragedy. And, once, again, to think that I'd consider, ever, asking her to be my wife: NEVER! Or, no doggone way! I say again: NO DOGGONE WAY…!

It's also good or even great…! That, I've never told my family, and especially, my mother, or *Zakira*, about her: Caren Colson. I would've lifted *Zakira* up—only, to be let right down, once, more; right, by the likes of yet another doggoned female loser: A sorry, stupid, and sick loser of a girl friend, or fiancée, or even wife—that, I just can't and won't appreciate—or, use. It's just not within my *character* to do so: Stoop, or bend, or even get down in the cess-pool, or the cess-pit with such a fantastically fallible female of a *femme fatale*.

NO, THANK YOU! I say again: No, thank you, to such a fantastically filthy fairytale of a dream, nightmare! That favorite highway of a restaurant is coming up…, near Orlando. My senses are being so awaken, again, in absolute anticipation of a deliciously good breakfast; which is going to fill me right up with *personal power* or staying power or even strength; rightly, to just flower pretty powerfully right through all the doggone mud. It's just the miserably messy mud, which usually placates or vacates dating and aching, both.

Still, I've to just carry on smartly, and strongly, and even successfully, some-how. It's what true character is all about, isn't it? Sticking, so soundly, or roundly, to a certain philosophy of life…, and the methodology by which I just live it—my life. Or, more, to the point, just, produce the necessary courage; rightly, to persevere, right, through my adversary commitment; and, rightly, to find, get, or have, and even keep the great love of my life. I trust, as well, that her aggregate traits, or qualities, or even habits, and all, will be of very good repute; which can't and won't be rebuked or refuted, ever, if so, hardly.

Yet, again, I've to just find such woman—or such lady. Therefore, I even speed up some more. Since, time is of the essence, here, still. ...I'm talking all about obtaining, retaining, plus maintaining a great measure of peace: plus, health, love, and happiness, and even success, if not rest...: plus, perseverance, commitment, and, courage, and, even, with some luck, honor. Or, get right through what's bad to get right to what's good or great: GREAT! The cute lizard that likes visiting me or keeping my company, at my home, in Naples, will help me.... HAW! HAW! HAW!

Seriously, I'll do it or get right to what's very good or even great. Do so, scrupulously, and, decisively, without a jaggedly broken heart—and woefully wasteful flowers...; both of which, just, can't help—but, to disintegrate into a doggonedly dark-naked state of dis-integration...: or, fall to doggoned pieces. Quite, simply, such isn't and hasn't been the *theme* or the scheme of things, here, ever. But, instead, to just keep my very vigilant eyes on the pretty potent prize whether elusive or not. Focus, now! Plus, get and then keep my *mood* or my *attitude* up, and, way!

For darn sure, that, it requires some true character—or, characterization; whose characteristics aren't just made up, symbolically, or even indefinably, just, like in a shadily sketchy character sketch; or, whose characterology isn't of any doggone consequence. Zip! ...POUND...! Abundantly, it's only the successful or the super sure sound of my hope, faith, ambition, and, strength, or, staying power: *personal power*, without any frown; all of which can never be bound, ever; right, to some type of scandalously loose-kissing and pussy-footing female of a fantastic clown; who dilly-dallies all around town—or even, on the ground, and all wound up. No, thank you...! I just say again: NO, THANK YOU...!

As, I'm not at all about having to school some doggonedly, or some poisonously pretty piss-tail gal, girl.

YES! That restaurant is now in view. Once, again, we're almost through, here, where upon I've been trying—only, to bring one of my best dreams to reality; or, even, trying to end one of my worst nightmares, in actuality. Or, better yet, I'm just about done constructing, and then de-constructing, then re-constructing this tantalizingly tall tell-tale of mine. …Hmmm…, I hum in super sheer delight. I'm delighted, and, quite. That a deliciously good breakfast will skew, further, any nakedly negative view—or, views, as it were: views of my out-playing, and out-working, and even out-standing—all, STILL!

…HMMMM…, I hum, yet again, at the tantalizing thought of such breakfast or big building blocks…. That're building right up my mind, heart, and body, and even spirit, for the big business meeting that I've tomorrow. ZIP! Move it…! Or, just, get out of my dog-gone way—slow-moving cars, (especially, today, or right now…)! I'm just moving to the far outer lane. Then, ZOOM…!

Or, BOOM…! It's only the super sheer, or the super sure sound of a pretty lone, yet palpable, and powerful, and even perfect, or very pinkish-black-colored flower. That's flowering, and fantastically, if not fabulously. Or, it's only blooming, and, most beautifully…! Now, there just needn't be any more dog-gone double-takes…; and, triple-takes…; or see-sawing…; or wig-wagging…; or zig-zagging…, and so forth. ZIP—ZOOM! Or, just, MOVE IT…!

Still, I look right up at the review mirror. Not, only, am I seeing a deeply dark-olive-colored male; whose very light-chest-nut-brown-shaded eyes; shapely brows; almond-shaped nose; curvy lips; high cheeks; wide shoulders; and all; represent, so very roundly, the very visual qualities of my very being; which so encompasses my mind, heart, and body, and even spirit, or soul, viscerally, and, very.

But, also, I'm just admiring the male or guy; who, almost, never, takes anything, anyplace, or anyone, at face-value; instead, so valuing what's in the inside as opposed to what's on the outside; or, on the surface; or, even, on the face of it—hers, Caren's, or whoever…. I'm just a super split image of my wonderfully wise mother and father—both. Indeed, my sister or Zara is even a super split image of our parents, and especially, my mother, or *Zakira*.

I look down at my clothing, denim, or shirt, and my pair of Levi's, pants; whose broad metal belt is encircling my totally tight torso. Plus, I look just as fine as I feel—fit, and fantastically. I'm even thinking all about this fittingly fantastic song by the very legendary singer, and all; or, Mr. Robert Dwayne "Bobby" Womack, (born in 1944…): "If You Think You're Lonely Now."

I just can't help—but, to play it on my car's serious-sounding stereo system…. Reaching right for the compact disc or, CD, that's right in my CD case; within a minute or so…, the super soulful sounds of the pretty poetic Bobby Womack sound out, soulfully, or, somewhat, suitably. And, before I forget…, the album is entitled, poetically, or, quite appropriately: *The Poet*.

Next, I'll more than likely listen to the rhythmically soulful sounds of New Birth's "Wild Flower," (and, …the long version); I'll find it, (wild flower)—or, her, soon, and, very: The most wonderful woman or lady; who, I'll be darn sure to shower, wildly, or, big-heartedly, with the loveliest of pink flowers or pretty pink roses. Plus, open-handedly, she'll be given my heart…. Presently, and, most ironically, I'm just so very thankful for my present single-ness, which will allow me to find such lady or such woman.

I'm grateful, as well, for my comfortably suitable shoes; or, my comfortably pitch-black, suede, and, beady moccasins that're all Indian-like. That're right on my pretty productive feet—or, on the darned go…: traveling high and low; or, just, going to and fro…, in a circularly careful or concerted or even concentrated effort; rightly, to just bring all of my deliciously—if not, my decidedly good dreams—right, to reality or actuality, still.

GO! Or better, just, keep moving…! ZOOM—ZIP! Or, better yet, just, produce, produce, and produce…: YES, SIRREE! I'm still producing, so productively, my own darn productivity or production of a definitely delicious dream. That wants and needs to come true, or alive, STILL!

I just start singing right out—right, along, with Mr. Womack…: "…If you think you're lonely now huh/ Wait until tonight, Girl/ (If you think you're lonely now)/ I'll be long gone…." And, that I am: or, so, long, gone. Or, even, GOOD-BYE, and GODDARNED GOOD RIDDANCE…! To, that darned licentious loser, user, or mis-user, or even god-darned abuser of a female…! Of course, I'm referring to Caren Colson, still. But, the still-ness or the solid-ness of some super solid food is right in sight….

Hmmm: Or, Yum-Yum! Those big bites of food are going to be quite good—or, GREAT, for darn sure…! HA! HA! HA! ZIP—ZOOM…! Or rather, I'm only hurrying, or traveling, or even journeying right on, or onwards, or even upwards. Though, I'm not at all oblivious of, or ignorant in knowing—that, it's some-times very necessary to journey or travel downwards: Do so, right, in order to greet or meet someone at her or his very lower level…; Just, the same, so concerning Caren Colson—NEVER!

Because, there are some pretty powerful standards that ought not—or, can't be negotiated, or placated, or even vacated—EVER! In other words, having prior knowledge all about Caren Colson's super sub-standard-ness has been, most definitely, like having real power. Plus, I just couldn't or wouldn't permit her to have such powerfully poisonous power right over me…. If so, I would've been nothing but a blunderingly blithering idiot or a buffoon! ZOOM—ZIP…! Or, more, to the point…, HMMMM—or, YUM, YUM…!